D0423724

YOU MUST BE THIS HAPPY TO ENTER

stories

Elizabeth Crane

PUNK PLANET BOOKS
Chicago

Published by Punk Planet Books/Akashic Books
©2008 Elizabeth Crane

Punk Planet Books is a project of Independents' Day Media.

Book design by Pirate Signal International
Cover photo by Daniel Sinker

ISBN-13: 978-1-933354-43-9
Library of Congress Control Number: 2007926133

First printing

Some of these stories previously appeared in the following publications: *The Banana King*: "Banana Love"; *Other Voices*: "Clearview" and "What Our Week Was Like"; *Punk Planet*: "Sally (Featuring: Lollipop the Rainbow Unicorn)"; FiveChapters.com: "What Happens When the Mipods Leave Their Milieu"; *After Anthology*: "Emmanuel"; Failbetter.com: "Promise"; *Ecotone*: "Varieties of Loudness in Chicago"; and *The Best Underground Fiction: Volume One*: "Blue Girl." "Donovan's Closet" was originally published as a Featherproof minibook. "You Must Be This Happy to Enter" was originally commissioned and broadcast by Stories on Stage in Chicago.

Punk Planet Books
PO Box 13050
Chicago, IL 60613
books@punkplanet.com
www.punkplanetbooks.com

Akashic Books
PO Box 1456
New York, NY 10009
info@akashicbooks.com
www.akashicbooks.com

For Nina,
I'm sorry I stole your hat.
Yours 'til Lois Lane.

CONTENTS

ACKNOWLEDGMENTS

- I acknowledge Bob, I am grateful to Lisa, and I idolize Megan.
- I recognize the value of Gina Frangello.
- I pay tribute to Amy Krouse Rosenthal, WBEZ, Kathe Telingator, and Alice Hoffman.
- I regard highly Alice Tasman and Reagan Arthur.
- I revere Anne Elizabeth Moore.
- I set great store by Dan Sinker.
- J'aime Daniel Arsand trois fois.
- I have never met Johnny Temple or Johanna Ingalls, but I want to, because I owe them plenty.
- Jessica Thebus, Laura Eason, and Steven Shainberg are visionaries, and I salute them.
- I just really like Jonathan Messinger.
- My family rules.
- I love Ben.

And now I have to confess the unpardonable and the scandalous
. . . I am a happy man.
　　　—Jean Cocteau

MY LIFE IS AWESOME! AND GREAT!

I! LOVE! MY LIFE! MY life is awesome and great! I have all the things anyone would ever want! I have awesome friends! I have an awesome partner for life! I have a window to look out of! It is under the roof that is over my head! You would love my life too if you had it, but you don't, because I do! I! Am not trying to say that I don't ever cry! Who could say that? No one but a very repressed person! That is why I would never say that! I am only trying to say that even though I sometimes cry, like when my aunt dies or when my awesome life partner is sad, that doesn't mean that my life isn't awesome and great, because it is! My life has many feelings and one of them is being sad! Being able to be sad when sadness comes is part of what makes my life so awesome and great! I have tried to be happy when I am sad and that has only made me sadder! And sometimes angry! So I don't do that anymore! You shouldn't either! It's unrealistic! If you are reading books like *How to Be Happy* or buying fancy stationery or bubble bath because you think it will make you happy, it won't! Don't do it! Fancy stationery is nice and so is bubble bath but these are special treats! Do not think they are anything more! They aren't! Plus, you cannot learn how to be happy from a book! Except if it's *Jonathan Livingston Seagull*! Then you can!

Let me tell you something else! I don't have lots of money! I'm not saying I wouldn't like more money! Send me some! I am just saying that sometimes when I have money I am happy and sometimes I am still sad and sometimes when I don't have money I am also sometimes happy and sometimes sad! Sometimes when I have money or when I don't, I feel jealous! Or suspicious! Or bemused! These are just a few of the many things that are part of my awesome and great life of feeling! You might ask, how can anyone be happy when there are so many problems in the world! And I would say, those things make me sad too! But I am still happy! You know that old cliché where if you don't eat your brussels sprouts your parents say something like, "There are children starving all over the world," and you're supposed to be grateful and eat your brussels sprouts, except usually it doesn't work and you just mope in your plate and push your brussels sprouts around so it seems like you're eating them gratefully and feeling sadness for the starving children worldwide but really you are neither eating them nor grateful? Well that is not me! I am grateful! Also I like brussels sprouts! They are actually quite flavorful, especially with lots of butter! Many things are good with lots of butter! Like artichokes!

You might be saying, "I cannot relate to your awesome and great life!" But listen to this! Not so long ago, on top of these awesome things, I also had a good job! Except I was fired! I was not feeling so good about that! I had feelings of rejection and uneasiness! Mixed with surprise! I thought I was a competent worker, but in my review they gave me only a seventy-three percent competence rating! Did that stop me from walking out of there with my stapler and my ivy plant and my head held high? No! I believe that my positive attitude alone put my competence rating at no less than eighty percent! And that is respectable! Most importantly, though, I am a person who sees opportunity in times of trouble, and I knew that this was the universe's way of telling me it was time to pursue my dream of being on reality television! You might say, "That is a foolish thought," but I would say, "Maybe, maybe not!" I believe that when you have a dream of being on reality TV, as I did, and a chance comes, you must take it! So I did!

Unfortunately, it is not as easy to become a star of reality television as you might think, but I did not let that stop me! My first choice was to go on that show where you race around the world! Called *Race around the World*! Wouldn't that be so much fun, I thought! But my life partner wasn't as into that as I was, so I didn't! Because it would not be so much fun to be on so many airplanes without him! This was when I remembered that I am an awesome singer! So I drove to the closest place where they had tryouts for *Be a Famous Star*! Which was not so close at all, it was all the way over in Gary, Indiana! That was sure interesting! You may not know that there are long lines of

people who try out for *Be a Famous Star*! But there are! Or that
it is very cold waiting in the long lines in the parking lot of the
U.S. Steel Yard in Gary, Indiana in March, but that doesn't stop
people from coming! Not even people in wheelchairs! Not all
of these people can sing, though, which I thought would be to
my advantage! But it really wasn't! Because the judges did not
think I looked like a famous star! One of the celebrity judges
said my voice was not bad! The mean one asked me if I was
planning to keep shopping at the Rainbow Stores! I thought
that was especially mean because what is wrong with the Rainbow Stores? They have good prices and contemporary styles! I
asked him if this competition was about looks or about music
and he laughed like I should know it was about looks! I boldly
asked him if I shopped somewhere besides Rainbow Stores
would they send me to Hollywood? And do you think he said
yes? No! I had more feelings of rejection, but remember when
I said there were people in wheelchairs? Well, one of them was
waiting for his brother to audition after me and he saw my look
of rejection and said "Sorry" to me and I thought, someone in a
wheelchair feels sorry for me? That can't be right! I asked him
why he was in a wheelchair and he said he had a rare disease
whereby he could not bump into anything or he would have
severe internal bleeding! I said, "That is so terrible! Have you
ever tried to go on that show where they give people miracle
cures?" And do you know what? He said to me, "You will not
believe this but I was rejected from that show!" And he was
right! I didn't believe it! And what else is unbelievable is remember he was consoling me! That was when I knew he was an

especially nice person! I said, "That does not make any sense! Who could need a miracle more than you?" And do you know what he said? He told me that they chose to go with a blind woman! A plain old blind woman! I said, "That does not seem very interesting!" He told me that she had also recovered from cancer and that gave her the edge! I said, "Too bad you didn't recover from cancer!" And he said, "I know, right?"

You might think I was pretty discouraged by this point, but I was not! Because there are lots of reality television shows! I tried out for many of them! And was uniformly rejected! Even by some game shows! Like the one where you go grocery shopping really fast! That has always seemed like a lot of fun to me! Also, I would like to guess which suitcase has the most money! That show is suspenseful! I even tried out for two whole shows where you have to eat bugs! And I do not think I would like that! That is how much I would like to be on TV! Thankfully you do not have to eat them on the tryouts! So that's good! But they too rejected me! Plus, my awesome life partner was not so happy that I was not spending my time trying to pursue a reality job, and was no longer so interested in hearing about my life's dream! We were experiencing some difficulties in our relationship during which I began to suspect that he was cheating. How I guessed this was by him coming home very late at night over and over again and calling me Rita which is not my name, and also we were getting a lot of hang-ups that said *Walker, Rita* on the caller ID, which was not the name of any friend of mine, which was when I got the idea to try to get on that reality show where they secretly investigate your life partner to see if they are cheating, and guess what? They chose me!

Of course, it is not so great when you discover that your life partner is cheating! I did not realize that on this show, *Catch a Cheating Partner*, they do not ever use people whose partners do not cheat! Those episodes go right into the trash! I was very saddened to discover that my awesome life partner, who I did not think was so awesome right then, had indeed taken up with someone else! Who in my opinion was a very trashy ho based on her clothing very obviously not coming from anyplace like the Rainbow Stores, more like the Rainy Day I'm a Ho Stores! Why I feel like I can say this is that when they showed me the videotape of Rita Walker totally making out with my life partner you could see that her skirt barely covered her tired old raggedy ass! More like Rita "Street" Walker if you know what I mean! The good news is that through the disappointing experience of becoming a reality TV star on *Catch a Cheating Partner*, I realized that being on television was not going to make me happy even though secretly I still wanted to try out for one more show that might turn out more positively, such as the one where you become an intern to a mogul with a weird beard! Because you can win a lot of money on that show *and* become famous! Except I didn't! Because when the casting director noticed my long resume of TV show tryouts and said something like, "I think you might be avoiding your real life," I suddenly saw that I did have a problem with avoiding real life! My life partner agreed to go to couples counseling and we became stronger than ever after I joined a recovery program for my reality issues! Thanks to my higher power I no longer feel that TV fame will solve all my problems today! Not even! I am now hoping to pursue the growing field of mystery shopping! Because it sounds like fun to go shopping for a job! And mysterious!

You may still be saying, "That is very exciting, but your life is still not so awesome and great!" But let me tell you that there was a time when I did not realize how awesome and great my life was! Sometimes it is not so easy to see during times of trouble like I just told you about! Sometimes you have to just be happy that a tiny cute bird lands on your windowsill! Both because of the bird's cuteness but also because of having a windowsill! That's not nothing! During this time I could often be heard crying to my therapist, "I don't know what to do!" Over and over! My therapist would say, "Do this!" or, "Do that!" and I would say, "No!" And for a time I remained unaware of the awesome greatness of my life!

You might be saying, "If I have a dream of being on reality TV, will I be in danger of addiction like you?" And I would say, "Not necessarily!"

You might also be saying, "What if I have clinical depression?" I would say to this, "That is not what I am talking about! Perhaps medication would be right for you! Try it!"

You might also be saying, "I live in a Third World country! Your life is bourgeois!" Which is a fancy word meaning you have money! And you would be right! If you live in a Third World country it is a whole different kind of hard for you! It is harder to see the beauty in a Third World country, I am sure! But it is there!

Sometimes when I cannot find a parking spot near my house, and I pass by spots that are too small for my car to fit in by about only one inch, I feel frustrated until I remember that I have a car and that it still goes! Then I feel a grateful feeling! Because of having legs to walk a few blocks to my house! I could probably use the exercise anyway! And no longer am I perturbed about the orange El Camino that's been parked in the same spot right in front of my house for many weeks with many tickets on it, which would be such a cool car if it ever went which it seems not to! Unless the guy who owns it just likes looking at it from his window! How would I know? Maybe it reminds him of the good old days when his dad used to let him ride in the back with his dog Sweeney; before his dad became suicidal and threw himself in front of a milk truck! Maybe he got it on eBay for three dollars! You don't know! Which brings me to my final point!

Let's say you have an orange El Camino that does not go and it seems obvious that you should feel distraught, especially if you do not have any other car that goes and unlike me you do not have two legs to walk to your house, you only have one! You would have a right to feel many things! You might feel anger toward people who do not have to hop on one leg! Why wouldn't you? You might feel resentful because of there being so many pairs of pants in the world with two legs in them! Or maybe you would feel so tired you wouldn't even try to hop anywhere and so you'd feel super lonely staying home watching two-legged people filling out their pants on TV all the time! You could feel many things that might all be of a despairing nature, and you could feel many other things of a joyful nature! Feelings aren't facts! That is an expression I heard! Here is a secret! You can choose to love your life even if or possibly even because you have a truck that does not go! This is the truth! Believe it!

BETTY THE ZOMBIE

BETTY THE ZOMBIE WANTS TO CHANGE. How her husband knows this is he asked her, and she said, "Eeeeeeeehhhh!" which he finally determined to mean yes. (There had been a long process of trial and error in understanding Betty's speech, but in a climactic moment under the covers, Betty's trademark shout sounded much like her response to his question.) Betty the zombie's husband, Ed, loves her very much, but finds it hard to help her meet her special needs while also not becoming a zombie himself.

The back story on Betty and Ed is they'd been high school sweethearts. Ed was the kind of average-looking guy no one noticed one way or another, the type who might have bumped up into handsome if he'd had any style at all, but he hadn't. Betty was pretty in that sort of way where there's nothing really wrong with her and nothing really outstanding about her, although she did have really shiny hair that she wore in a nice flip. She thought it was shiny because she used Prell but really it was just because. Ed had the locker next to Betty's and noticed her shiny hair one day and she noticed that he was in the A.V. club, which she thought was really cool, which gives you an idea of both Betty and Ed. Even Ed knew A.V. wasn't cool. Ed was also really into race walking, which Betty did know wasn't cool, but she appreciated that he was physically fit. Betty and Ed continued on to Lombard Junior College where Ed dropped out after one semester to go into the family business of rivets even though he had hoped to someday pursue being a television producer. It sounded exciting, although Ed never did know exactly what that meant or how to go about it, and a search of the *Tribune* classifieds that turned up nothing proved enough to discourage him back into rivets. Betty transferred from LJC to a secretarial school because she was told by her mother that every girl should have typing to fall back on. Betty didn't have much of an idea at that time of what she wanted to fall forward onto, and felt some resistance to the idea of typing for a living, but didn't have any better plans. Plus she was a good girl so she usually did what her mom said even if it made her a little bit bitter inside.

They were married at the Lombard County Courthouse as soon as Betty graduated from typing school. Betty wore a cream-colored maxi-dress she crocheted herself and Ed wore sandals and a daisy in his lapel. That tells you what era it was. It sounds like they might have been hippies but they weren't. They were peace-loving, but you'd hardly have caught them marching anywhere, ever. They just wouldn't have thought of it. Ed, at this time, may have worn sandals to his wedding, but he was also still using Brylcreem.

Betty and Ed tried to have kids right away and they kept trying for a long time, and the long and short of it is that it just never happened. One time Betty missed her period and gained ten pounds and they were hopeful, but it was for naught. It was only because Betty really liked Pringles. They stacked. Betty learned to knit during this time and knitted a lot of hats and booties but mostly she just accumulated a lot of yarn, and then she accumulated a lot of hats and booties that were never to be worn. But still Betty and Ed were more or less happy, considering their childlessness. They got a dog and that helped a little. They called him Boone.

How Betty became a zombie was when another zombie took a bite out of her as she was digging through the remnant bin at JoAnn's Fabric and Crafts. Although Betty and Ed were aware of a recent outbreak of zombies downstate, this woman did not look to Betty like a zombie, so when the woman took this bite out of her she was quite alarmed. At first Betty and Ed did not put it together. Lombard, Illinois was a typically unremarkable suburb. There had been no reports of zombies anywhere in the greater Chicagoland area even, so they at first assumed this woman, who was never caught, had simply been insane. Betty went to the doctor and he stitched up the bite and prescribed some antibiotics, but it wasn't long before the wound began to fester and grow, and when Ed would say, "What do you want for dinner," Betty was having to fight the impulse to tell her husband that what she wanted most for dinner involved a big heaping portion of Ed. So, instead, for a while they ate a lot of steak and Betty would eat hers "rare," which Ed happened to notice was more like if Betty had taken the steak and waved it over the grill for a second, at a height of two feet.

What was bad was when one of the little neighbor boys went missing and a few days later Ed found a little neighbor boy–sized striped T-shirt in their laundry, which was when he began to suspect that Betty might be responsible. When he finally confronted her, she tried to act like it was no big deal. "He was so ssshmmall," she said. "I didn't think anyone would missh him." Except her eyes said she knew it really was a big deal. It was at this time that Ed also noticed the slight slurring of her speech.

Ed started sleeping in the den, which was when Betty started looking through the Yellow Pages for a therapist. She called a number of them but could not find any that specialized in zombies. While Ed was sleeping in the den was when he saw the show *Relight the Fire of You* on Lifetime and got the idea for Betty to go on the show. On this show seven women with problems to solve are chosen to live in a mansion in sunny Miami Beach, Florida. What they do is they pair the women up with life coaches. A big thing is they also have to deal with each other. *Because women aren't always nice, but they are always you*, the breathy voiceover says during the soft-focus montage at the beginning of the show, as though it actually means something. Sometimes they offer the women traditional therapy on an as-needed basis. Also, the life coaches give them group challenges and individually designed exercises just for each woman and her particular problem. Also, the life coaches hire a variety of "experts" to come in and help them with these problems. An expert being defined here as "someone who does something." Because *like a flower no two women are alike* (also from the montage) and as follows no two problems are alike and therefore no two solutions should be alike, is what the producers of this show seem to think. What happens is the women stay in the house and work on the problems for however long it takes and so people come and go except or until it's the end of the TV season and then they're S.O.L. Then they have to take the summer off like the crew and come back in the fall.

Ed drives Betty into Chicago for a casting call at the Marriott. There are probably a thousand people waiting to be seen by the casting directors, but as soon as her number comes up, by way of introducing herself, Betty barely has to say, "Beaaaaaaah!" before she's cast right away. *Relight the Fire of You* is currently not getting such good ratings and they have never had a woman with a zombie problem before, which they expect will be a draw. Betty and Ed have a somber goodbye, but agree that it's the best thing for both of them.

There are already six women in the house when Betty the zombie comes in. This group of women has issues of: severe clutter, overspending, being unable to gain weight, loneliness, prostitution, and murdering. And a few combinations thereof, such as Betty the zombie also has a murdering problem due to her dietary needs, but not because she likes murdering, really. She likes it when she eats, but she suffers remorse. Betty and Ed are sworn to secrecy about the neighbor boy and are thus far not suspected, as the prime suspect in the neighbor boy's disappearance is a creepy uncle in Ohio who hasn't been seen lately either. Besides the boy, Betty swears to Ed that she has only eaten live animals. "Raaaaaaaaaysh!" she will explain, meaning to say, "Strays," hoping that the eating of stray cats and dogs is somehow not as bad as eating pets with owners, or children. Still, Ed has been keeping a close eye on Boone.

On the day that a newcomer enters the house they do what they call a "greeting," which is where the newcomer tells the reason why they're there. This is hard for Betty because she has so much trouble talking. She will also get speech therapy. For the time being, during group activities, Betty has been provided with a zombie translator. The translator, not a zombie herself, but whose parents are zombies, has come to have a fine understanding of the nuances of most zombie dialects, as well as an obvious empathy. Betty moans and groans a lot and the zombie translator explains that Betty has come primarily because of the marital issues that have arisen as a result of her being a zombie and also because of her desire not to eat any more pets.

Betty's roommate is the girl who can't gain weight. She's a pretty sweet girl, nineteen, tall and thin, obviously, but guess what, nobody feels sorry for her because most of them have issues of being unable to lose weight, and so they kind of hate her, which is a big part of her problem both in and out of the mansion. "Boo hoo" and "Poor you" are the sorts of things they say to her no matter whether she's talking about having to buy clothes in the kids department or her alcoholic mother and sexually abusive stepbrother. This girl, Linda, is a good pairing with Betty for the obvious reason of her having nothing much to offer Betty in the way of being something she'd ever want to eat. But also because Linda is so sweet, and although Betty has the severely advanced speech problems at this point whereby it's hard to tell what her feelings are toward anyone, Linda correctly has the sense that Betty does not hate her. How she can tell this is Betty pats her on the head before they go to sleep. Betty patting someone on the head is kind of like when a two-year-old pats a dog, no control over the arms and more like hitting than patting, but Linda senses the intention and smiles and Betty makes a noise something like, "Oooo-aaaaii," that Linda takes to mean good night, even if it doesn't.

The life coach assigned to Betty asks her to clarify what her goals are, both inside the mansion and for after her "reignition," which is their term for when someone leaves the house. The translator ascertains for the life coach that Betty has a goal of not desiring to eat her husband or her dog and getting in touch with her childhood passion for sewing and other needle crafts, possibly starting a business. Betty the zombie's life coach gives her the assignment of choosing two pieces of fabric from a large selection of colors and patterns and then sewing them together, and she is to do this with one simple seam on a sewing machine. Important aspects of this exercise being both what the color and pattern choice say about her and also how straight she gets her seam. Betty chooses a lovely blue toile with a coordinating solid blue, which suggest to the life coach a desire for stability balanced with a touch of melancholy as represented by the color blue, and her seam is impressively straight except for it is sewn directly onto her hand. "Alright," says the life coach (who, just for a better picture, is fiftyish and has a largeish if obviously natural bosom that is usually offset by one of a variety of low cut, brightly colored tops from Forever 21), acting as though anyone's ever seen this before, saying, "Good, let's just move on," and endeavors to use a seam ripper to remove the fabric from Betty's hand, with grisly results. Betty moans and pulls away, leaving bits of her palm in the hand of her life coach.

Betty's initial daily group encounter is not much more productive. Most of the women are visibly uncomfortable with Betty and even the murderer thinks herself better. It might be noted that Gloria, the murderer, ran over her husband with their lawn mower, and had wanted to plead not guilty but instead took a plea bargain (serving nine years and now trying to reenter society and engage in new relationships via online dating) when strong evidence showed her malicious intent. Nevertheless, she feels entitled to judge other murderers and when she comments about the grotesque nature of Betty's appetite, Betty groans something like, "Ouuaahhhhhh!" and then under her breath (which for a zombie tends not to be subtle), "Behhhh," which the zombie translator explains means, "I can't help it!" and "Bitch." Sweet underweight Linda tries to come to Betty's defense and Gloria tells her to shut her skinny ass up.

Ruthann, the woman with the clutter issue, is annoying her roommate, Connie, the woman with the overspending issue, who doesn't have a problem with clutter because among many other things, she has spent a lot of money at The Container Store. Ruthann has the unique ability to enter a tidy room and dismantle everything in it in a manner of minutes. It simply does not occur to her to "put it back where you found it, bitch-ass slob," even though that's exactly what Connie says to her about every six seconds, because although she has no problem with clutter, she does take issue with those who clutter her space. All that occurs to Ruthann is to leave it wherever and to wonder why anyone cares. The life coaches have suggested to Ruthann that she is metaphorically "leaving" pieces of herself behind in the items she scatters in her wake; Ruthann so far isn't hearing this and maintains only that she is in the house because her apartment was declared uninhabitable by the health department, and that if it were up to her, the lifestyle of clutter would suit her "sense of freedom" just fine. Betty the zombie ends up identifying with Connie the overspending woman because when Connie asks Betty exactly what she had gone to JoAnn's for (lustily, like a sober drunk asking for details of a bender), Gloria points out that it seems as though Betty might have spent a pretty penny at JoAnn's that day had she not been intercepted by the zombie who bit her. As it was, Betty had gone to JoAnn's Fabric and Crafts directly from her other favorite store, Costco, where she had spent in the vicinity of three hundred dollars, which if you've never been to Costco is more or less enough to fill Betty and Ed's two-car garage. Betty and Ed do have a big home with lots of storage in the basement, and so she buys stuff on special and often in bulk telling herself she's saving money when really they will probably in their entire lives never use all the toilet paper in their basement, and that's just the toilet paper, we're not even getting into the craft supplies that have long occupied the entire attic, and, truth be told, Betty kind of likes the feeling she has inside the cavernous walls of Costco, like she's a part of something larger than herself, like if she picks up enough four-packs of Crest, a part of Costco will be with her. So via the translator Betty discovers that her issues are even more complex than she had originally believed. Unfortunately, once you become a zombie you have a whole new set of issues above and beyond overspending, and there's no known antidote to being a zombie although there are new and exciting ways of coping with being a zombie that are emerging daily. Many of them involve specially designed garments to conceal and contain wounds from growing worse during typical daily activities. One possibility that is presented is that of medication, but Betty rejects this option because she does not want the possible side effects of weight gain and decreased sexual appetite. (Never mind that Ed's sexual appetite has dropped off considerably due to Betty's perpetually open wounds being something he can't quite get around. Almost literally. Ed and Betty had enjoyed a healthy sex life when her arms and legs could bend without breaking, but at this point, Ed can only bring himself to make love to his wife if she is completely clothed, which is obviously problematic, and on the rare occasion since then that they've tried anything other than missionary style, the ensuing pops and cracks tend to dampen Ed's mood.)

Rolonda, the woman with severe loneliness, shares the large master bedroom with both Gloria the murderess and also Marny, the woman trying not to be a prostitute, which again is thought by the life coaches to be opposite enough to get the women to deal with their issues together. Marny the prostitute is not shy, right, neither is Gloria the murderess as we've already seen. Rolonda simply finds it hard to be in the same room as someone else. She would be as lonely at the Super Bowl as she would in an isolation tank.

Soon after Betty's arrival, for an exercise in "group dynamics," the women are gathered for a game of *Electric Fence Limbo*, which is exactly what it sounds like. Each round, the electrified limbo pole is lowered until all of the women are eliminated. Betty loses in the first round when the pole is at neck height, due to her extremely limited ability to bend any part of herself, and when she senses (by way of a creak audible to the entire group) that she's close to snapping her head straight off, she forfeits before her feet are barely under the pole. Gloria, somewhat overweight, suffers a severe burn to her stomach, and is the second woman out. The others fall to the ground one by one and Linda is the final woman to go under; however, "There are no winners in the game of limbo," the life coaches announce after it's over, "only players." "What the hell does that mean?" Ruthann asks "What do you think it means?" the life coach replies. "I don't think it means shit," Ruthann says. "I think it means Gloria got electrocuted on TV." "Mmm," says the life coach, nodding and squinting her eyes like she's thinking except she really isn't. "Interesting . . ." which is what she says when she gets caught but wants people to think she's making the women think for themselves. Betty wishes to herself that she'd known all of this before she played since she'd rather be a loser than take the chance that she'll lose her head entirely.

Anyway, this is still about Betty the zombie but it's important to know a little about what we're dealing with because each of these women has some pretty deep-seated problems, and as it turns out Betty will not be the last to be reignited. Gloria, for one, has some resistance to admitting her murdering problems, and Marny has solicited several members of the crew and one groundskeeper since entering the mansion, not to mention that she is deep in debt because her "agent" (previous remark from Gloria to Marny regarding this word: "I think that dude was called a pimp last time I checked") takes seventy percent and also because she has a habit of buying clothes instead of doing laundry. (Snippet of previous conversation between Gloria and Marny about this problem: "What if you drop it off?" "I don't want people touching my lingerie." "Um, you're a whore." "At least I'm not a murderer." "Whatever." "Whatever, I don't kill people." "So you say." "You'd best step off, beeyotch." "Whatever.") Rolonda often stays in her room.

So this particular cast remains on this show for a long time, and it's not an accident that the ratings go up after Betty joins them. Betty's fan e-mail box becomes full as soon as her first episode airs, not a few of these messages being from other women who struggle with zombie-related issues but also from non-zombie women who say they learned that zombies weren't just undead but that they have feelings too. Betty makes an effort to answer a few e-mails but breaks off her left pinky finger on the shift key and instead has the translator post a note to all her fans thanking them for their support and telling them that it means a lot.

There are times when Betty—who was always a pretty nice person and is still, in spite of her situation—feels patronized by the life coaches. She rightly perceives the harsh judgment

on the part of the ones who say that they aren't judging her because, "That's totally not what this show is about,"but really she
can tell that they are judging her because of them being all, "Are
you sure you really want to change? Because honestly it doesn't
matter to us," at which time Betty gets in touch with some of
her anger. Betty openly mocks the tone of the life coach to her
face, knowing that the coach cannot understand her, and that
the zombie translator won't give her away.

Betty has a few setbacks in the house, like the night she
sleepwalks into the master bedroom and is about to snack on
Ruthann, the clutter woman, who also has a weight issue, until
Rolonda with the loneliness spies her and shoos her out of the
room with a shotgun (for which she receives a star on account
of this being an important step in her dealing with other people;
"Violence is an attempt to connect," the life coach says to the
camera). Each of the women (except for Gloria the murderess,
for obvious reasons) had been given a shotgun upon Betty's en-
try into the mansion, although the weapons are actually loaded
with blanks and serve only to shoo Betty away, and, of course,
Betty is unaware of this, since it wouldn't work very well if she
were. But there's also a rotation of armed guards on set with
Betty in the event that she does need to be rekilled for the protection of the cast and crew.

The issue of Betty's diet is a much-debated problem. In
spite of a steady regimen of freshly deceased strays provided by
the pound, and although she has been making great advances
through group therapy (the translator has learned that Betty
is somewhat trainable, much like a dog, and can be distracted

away from a housemate next to her in the circle with the tasty paw of a newly dead kitten), Betty continues to try to sneak into her housemate's rooms at night for a taste of human. She comes close to the bedside of Gloria the murdering woman, who has taken Ruthann's gun and is most dismayed to discover that her effort to rekill Betty results in nothing, due to the blanks, and although the guard shoots Betty in the back, this too results only in a spray of shoulder all over Gloria and loud moan from Betty as they remove her from the room. A nutritionist is brought in who proposes that Betty's jaw be wired shut for the safety of everyone, and that she be fed a puree of blood and cow brains mixed with vitamins. Betty reluctantly agrees but has some concerns about how the jaw-wiring will affect her future sex life with Ed, not yet knowing that Ed isn't really into getting a blowjob where there's a chance that lips and tongue will be left behind on his dick anyway.

Eventually Connie the overspender calls Betty out on her underlying issue of compulsive shopping and Betty is sent to a twelve-step group with Connie, which is a breakthrough for Betty. Over time she comes to realize that she had never properly mourned the loss of not having children. Sobbing loudly and trying to talk at the same time, Betty says, "OOOHH-HAAAAYYYIII BOOOOOO DAAAAAAHH!!!" Which the translator explains to the group is Betty saying, "Sometimes when Ed goes to work, I put the booties on the dog." Due to Betty's childlessness and plus Boone the dog not being an entirely satisfactory baby substitute, she has been trying to fill a hole in herself with anything and everything. One life coach muses, "And isn't it interesting how you manifested these holes in this other way . . ." to which Betty thinks to tell the man to bite her, because even though she concedes that being in the mansion is a good thing, she can get kind of irritated with the whole metaphor thing they seem to be all about. Betty has unwittingly quit shopping cold turkey and understandably has been in the middle of complete withdrawal in the weeks since she became a zombie, which has exacerbated her overall problem. Now that Betty has taken the first step in admitting to the group her "Ouaaalaaamaaaa!" (powerlessness) over shopping, she already feels a certain freedom, and that night in group she receives her first gold star, ten of which add up to reignition. Through this revelation Betty comes to see that she is cross-addicted, recognizing her particular food issues as another thing she is powerless over, and this is the true beginning of her relighting-the-fire-of-you.

However, speech and physical therapy prove more difficult for Betty the zombie. Although her movement becomes slightly less stiff over time, her ability to express herself when the translator is unavailable is so impaired that she has learned to master a specially designed oversized keyboard that she can utilize without severing digits, and which has various special programs, one that allows her to write e-mail through an advanced and complex use of emoticons and one that translates her thoughts into a sort of robotic speech. Betty has a fight with Rolonda over use of the computer, resulting in another star for Rolonda, being as this is one of the only ways Rolonda connects with anyone, even if it is inmates at a maximum security prison (which she is told by the life coaches that she identifies with because she is trapped in the prison of herself). This fight is actually progress for both Betty and Rolonda, because Rolonda doesn't run to her room and Betty is able to communicate "Maiiiii tuuuuhhh" to Rolonda, which is one of the first times Betty is correctly understood using her own words by anyone in the house.

This is a wonderful day for Ed. Her first message is a voice e-mail to her husband that says, "I love you so much, Ed. Thank you for not leaving me, Ed," in a computer-generated mono-tone, and as she writes it she begins to shed her first tears since leaving Ed for the house, but this unfortunately ends up being rather messy as a good bunch of eye goo comes along with it.

Now that she has made some significant emotional prog-ress, for practical matters, as an exercise in developing her ar-tistic interests, Betty is enrolled in a papermaking class, which goes fairly well until she mashes her elbow through the screen. By this time, given the issues Betty has with losing parts of her-self, she is fitted with special gloves coated in Teflon that allow her more range of motion without further injury.

At this point Betty has eight stars, which is when a house-mate gets a makeover, usually a sign that she is coming close to reignition. Betty is excited about this because she has been especially self-conscious about her hair, which not long ago had been so shiny, but is now dull and unruly. She's not handy with a brush and cannot wash her hair by herself at all, and has ex-tremely dark circles under her eyes, which are remedied quite easily in her makeover with a heavy concealer. She looks passable at first, from ten feet or from behind you might never suspect her condition, and the simplest possible grooming routine has been designed for her, but she will have to practice a lot to keep it up. On one of her first tries, a mascara wand gets stuck in her forehead, at which point it occurs to one of the consultants to just have Betty's eyelashes dyed. She is also given an entirely new wardrobe of clothes custom-made with Velcro closures for easier dressing. Which comes none too soon, as Betty finds it easier to remain in one outfit until it reeks than to take the chance of breaking off a limb trying to pull a sweater over her head. She gets a ninth star when she completes an oven mitt without sewing herself to anything in the process.

But Betty the zombie is unable to get a tenth star for months, in spite of nothing but positive progress. The truth is that the producers of the show don't want her to reignite because she's so popular, which she finds out by overhearing a crew member. Betty then threatens to quit, explaining that she needs to get back to Ed and move on with her life and that she really doesn't care whether she "reeeaggahhhh" (reignites) or not because she's ready to leave, whatever you want to call it. The producers send Betty a fruit basket in the hope that she will consider staying on just a while longer until perhaps they find another zombie with issues, but the basket wouldn't have changed her mind even if it had had Pringles in it, which it hadn't.

Betty makes a call to Ed who makes a call to a lawyer who makes a call to the producers to basically tell them that because of their using Betty the way they did they need to do a little better than a fruit basket, like let's just say you should think about giving Betty a spin-off or we will sue your asses five ways from Beelzebub. After much discussion, the producers finally realize that giving Betty a spin-off could result in lots of money for them, which is when Ed and Betty's lawyer writes it into the new contract that Ed will be given a coproducer credit, which is pretty much a happy ending for both Betty and Ed and the producers. Betty the zombie will host a zombie craft talk show. Sometimes there will be celebrity guests and other zombies who will share their crafting techniques and ideas. It's an exciting time for everyone.

Because of this, Betty comes to believe that there are no accidents in life—or, in her case, undeath—and that the reason she was bitten by the zombie in the first place was to deal with her preexisting issues of overspending and not having children. In her twelve-step work there has been much discussion about hitting a bottom, which Betty has come to realize was putting herself in a position to be bitten by a zombie at JoAnn's Fabric and Crafts. Now Betty feels that this has created the important life purpose of being able to share her experience, strength, and hope with other zombies and even the fully alive, through her passion for crafts.

BANANA LOVE

SHE IS NEWLY MARRIED. SHE has many reasons to believe this marriage is an exceptionally good one. They jump up and down at the door when one comes back after an overnight trip out of town. They invent silly songs about making guacamole and asparagus pee and how the trash bags always break and about Zoloft and pretentious modern art and whatever else comes into their heads to sing about. They believe in god, they make love often, they hardly ever fight, and when they do fight there's hardly any yelling and it's always fair. They travel well together, although credit is due to the husband, she thinks, because she does not travel well alone. They split up the chores and say nice things all day every day. This is what marriage is to her so far. But, for comparison, she really has nothing. This is her longest romantic relationship ever. She has not been married before. She has observed marriage from the vantage point of daughter, friend, sister, and occasional reader of US Weekly. Some of these marriages seem successful, some obviously not. All of these marriages appear different, even the successful ones. It seems impossible to her to conduct any kind of scientific study based on any compilation of numbers. She's heard the numbers, and read an article recently that claimed that some of the numbers have been wrong the whole time. It seems impossible to determine the definition of success by anything numerical, e.g., the divorce rate. Couldn't there be some couple out there who divorced who did not consider their marriage a failure? Even if, she supposes, there were a study in which married participants charted the monthly number of miscommunications, lovemaking, compliments and/or loving sentiments, chores performed per spouse per day, quality time spent, agreement-to-disagreement ratio, etc., there would still be incalculable variants preventing a succinct definition of marriage that could be universally agreed on. Plus, it seems obvious to her that when a marriage ends, it is not widely regarded as having been a successful one, though she suspects this is a matter of perspective. She suspects, of course, that in many ways everything comes down to perspective. She has never been so interested in marriage until this time. She has previously gone out of her way to avoid conflict of any kind, with only marginal success. She has not been to outer space, which she feels is a location where there may be no conflict. She is willing, we should say, to entertain and perhaps even accept the idea that some conflict exists even in the best of relationships. If you told her a story that began, "Once upon a time there was a couple who agreed on every single thing that could possibly ever come up except for he liked bananas and she found them frightening," she would almost believe it. If the story went that they both liked dark chocolate (never milk), abundant cacti (never jade plants), cilantro (never parsley), Brooklyn (never Manhattan), the old seedy Times Square (never the new clean Times Square), hardwood floors with area rugs (never wall-to-wall carpeting), that eating microwave popcorn is like eating mulch, that sugar has gotten way too bad of a rap all around, that the word *blog* is too hard to say, that there are too many acronyms in the world these days for anyone's good; that they agreed you don't have to finish a book if you don't like it, that a little bit of reality television never hurt anyone but that the History Channel is the best thing ever invented, that there should be a new American revolution in which they themselves lead an uprising that begins on the Brooklyn Bridge and gathers people all the way to California and back to the White House where they outnumber all the existing police, military, and national guard, or whatever and park on the lawn for however many weeks it takes for the government to pull out of the dumbass war (and for just one example, this was something they discovered they had in common when they started dating, when the wife happened to mention her plan by saying something like, "Wouldn't it be nice if we could . . ." and the husband practically proposed right there and then, so freaked out was he at her articulating his deepest fantasy), that they agreed to change exactly the same number of diapers per child per day, they agreed to spend time with their in-laws even though the wife's parents only ever served leftovers that could never be traced back to any definable origin and the husband's mother was a vicious gossip and an occasional very bad klepto (she had a habit of swiping things that were too big not to notice, such as a particularly large piece of pottery the wife had brought back from a trip to Mexico, and would tend to do this while other people were in the room), and that this couple agreed, in the event of a disagreement, to disagree, she would believe this as well. She would not be surprised if the story went that this couple spent most days loving each other like lunatics but that every now and then the husband would forget and bring a banana into the house, sending the wife deep into the mental anguish of her childhood when she was forced to eat brown bananas because her parents would never waste anything, and the husband would apologize but also try to get her to work through the banana issue, and the wife would try to work through the banana issue but it would stretch itself out over the life of their marriage. It would not be unbelievable to our original woman that this other husband would start by bringing only something with something representing a banana, like maybe a Curious George book, which is not at all about bananas but occasionally will include a banana image. To which the wife would then say, "Okay, I see that's not so bad," and then in the future sometime, not too soon, the husband would be allowed to move ahead into bringing something banana-flavored into the house, like banana bubble gum maybe, and the wife wouldn't even have to chew it so much as tolerate it. And then the following year maybe a banana chocolate chip muffin, but only if it was banana-flavored and not made with real bananas because this wife knew that real banana baked goods were often made with overripe fruit. Maybe the wife would even take a bite of the banana chocolate chip muffin and say that it wasn't bad before she said, "Let's not bring anything else banana in here for a while." And so there would be years of banana-free living, at least at home, and even outside the home the wife would be careful to avoid possible banana sightings. At the grocery store, she would avoid the produce section altogether, leaving that disturbing errand to the husband, and if he happened to mention that he'd eaten a banana at work, she'd ask him to please not talk like that around her. "Even if it was a perfectly yellow, blemish-free fruit, I don't need to be imagining what happened to the peel in your office. A banana peel has no place in a work environment." (And "The trash?" was not the right answer.) She would deny the very existence of *National Geographic*, "a periodical practically devoted to bananas," she called it, and she would avoid any movies involving simian creatures of any kind, from *King Kong* (all versions) to *Gorillas in the Mist* to the seemingly harmless *George of the Jungle*, and certainly *Spanking the Monkey* despite assurances from her husband that there was not even one monkey in the movie, much less a banana. Naturally, she would have nothing to do with Josephine Baker or even Carmen Miranda. If there was any hint that bananas might be present on any given occasion, she would have the husband investigate in advance, and it is important to note that plantains were also out of the question. Needless to say, in spite of the absence of bananas in either their fashion or their décor, she did not shop at Banana Republic. She did not need to be reminded. Occasionally, if she was in an especially good mood, she could tolerate her husband serenading her with a single chorus of, "Yes, We Have No Bananas." Once, however, on a seemingly innocuous visit to P.S.1 to see a show of New York artists, she stumbled upon a hideously realistic and rather large C-print of a peeled, entirely black banana, pretty much her worst nightmare, and had a panic attack right in front of it, blaming her husband, who should have known. In between each of the banana moments there would be years of their crazy, agreeable love for each other, but it would always come back up sooner or later, because the husband really loved bananas and didn't want to keep his banana love a secret, eating them in the car in the dim light of the garage as he would, feeling shame about eating something no one should really have to feel shame about eating, like let's say if he was eating his own poo there in the car, and so he would eventually and tentatively ask his wife if, because he was feeling this unfitting shame, maybe it wasn't time to bring some sort of banana item into the house, like a frozen chocolate-covered banana, which in retrospect he should have known was a grievous miscalculation on account of we're dealing with an actual banana which is hidden, and concealed underneath the chocolate coating could be an unthinkably brown banana. Which would lead to maybe their biggest conflict ever, with the wife saying, "No, it wasn't that time at all," and, "How could you not see that?" The wife would continue, "Even a plain underripe real banana would have been better than a chocolate-covered banana." And the husband would try to understand and he would apologize but he would also say, "This is ridiculous!" because it's been years of this banana thing for him even though "This is ridiculous!" is never a thing to say to your

wife even when it is, and he feels and says that much more attention has been paid to her banana-avoidance issue than to his
banana-loving issue, to which she feels and says, "Of course
more attention has been paid to my banana-avoidance issue
than to your banana-loving issue, because banana-loving is *not an
issue*." And then they talk about going to couples counseling because each of them feels misunderstood, and then they do go to
couples counseling and the couples counselor encourages them
to remember what they had known decades ago, which is that
there isn't really a right or wrong when it comes to the subject
of bananas, and the couples counselor, who is working on her
thesis, can see that they agree on everything else and publishes
a lengthy article about their astonishing compatibility on everything but this one thing, and the couple ends up laughing about
it and they know for sure that the banana issue has been worked
through because one day they have a potluck picnic and a neighbor brings a red Jell-O mold exclusively with bananas inside and
the wife can pretty much see that these bananas, while mostly
fine, are not entirely spotless, and what ends up happening is
that when the neighbor comes in offering the Jell-O with bananas inside, the couple look at each other and then realize that
not just the husband is reaching to take the Jell-O but so is the
wife, at which gesture they simultaneously toss their heads back in
laughter, at which time there would be a freeze-frame on them
tossing their heads back in laughter, like really this whole story was
a '70s sitcom the whole time. Not forgetting our original wife, the
newlywed, hearing this story, feels she doesn't really know anything more than she ever did about marriage.

NOTES FOR A STORY ABOUT PEOPLE WITH WEIRD PHOBIAS

THERE'S A TALK SHOW.

- The host is "a regular guy."
- He has a New York accent. Or: a faint Boston accent, but not the Waspy kind.
- Host wears sweaters indicating regularness.
- Host's hair is thick and lush, slightly less than newscastery, but he is neither especially handsome nor unhandsome.
- He is fifty years old. Or: fifty-two.
- The title of this episode is, "Help! I'm Afraid of Wool!" It is about people with unusual phobias of seemingly innocuous things, maybe even things most people think are cute.
- Like say bunnies. The people seem completely genuine about these phobias, shaking even as they speak about them. Friends and family members attest to veracity of

phobias and encroachment of phobias on lives of friends and family members.

• Other things people are afraid of on this episode: balloons, birds, clowns, milk, the front door, and the sky.

A SCENE: Host spends a few minutes talking to each phobic guest about the nature of their particular phobia.

Why would you be afraid of balloons? host says, in that tone that says, *That's crazy*. That's crazy! he says.

They're going to kill me someday, I know it, the guest replies.

What? asks the host. How?

I don't know, he or she says. There's just going to be a lot of them.

What is it about them that's scary to you? the host goes on, with the *that's crazy* tone.

I don't like the way they're all . . . floaty, the guest says with a shiver.

Joe or Phil, the host calls offstage to a producer or intern, bring in the balloons!

Producer/intern Joe/Phil brings in a big bunch of helium balloons. Closer and closer to the guest.

Guest runs all around the room screaming.

STYLE: Omniscienty narrator. Something about this being really really cruel on the part of the regular-seeming host.

• Qs: Why would he do this? Why would anyone? Host seems so nice. Why am I watching this? That poor lady/guy—Could this *possibly* help anyone? Maybe it's just entertainment? Do they warn guests that there might be a bunch of balloons, etc.? Why agree to come on show with possibility of balloons etc.? Why do people want to be on television anyway? Phobia vs. fear: discuss.

SEVERAL SCENES: More segments with more guests and more weird phobias:

- Birds.

> Host: Birds? *All* birds?
>
> Guest: Newborn birds are alright.
>
> Host: Why birds?
>
> Guest: Birds are twitchy and fluttery, they are evil demons who want to eat us. Guest carries birdseed everywhere to "toss one way so she can run the other."

- Milk.

> Host: Well, a lot of people don't like milk. I don't really like milk, but I'm not scared of it.
>
> Guest: You should be. Guest says anything that comes in contact with milk must be washed an even number of times or thrown away.
>
> Host: What about a milk carton?
>
> Guest: Don't even.

- The front door.

> Host: Which side?
>
> Guest: Both sides!
>
> Host: Everyone has a front door!
>
> Guest: Not everyone.
>
> Host: What do you have instead?

Guest: A nice sheet.

Host: What if you get robbed?

Guest: I'd rather be robbed.

• Wool.

Guest: It's scratchy. It will choke you.

Host (*weary now, rolls his eyes*): If you say so.

• Clowns.

Host (*always with incredulous tone*): Clowns? Come on.

Guest: Look at them!

Host has brief second where astute viewer can see he may concede on this one. Guest checks windows and doors every morning and night.

Host (*snarky*): In case a clown comes by.

Guest: You don't know.

• The sky.

Guest: It's big and it's everywhere.

Host: You can't avoid the sky!

Guest: Oh yes I can.

—Host brings in more trays full of whatever the people are afraid of. A picture of the sky.

—Most of the guests run around the room screaming. One stays in chair, head in lap. Seems real. Unlike professional wrestling.

—Host says to one of them, Stop shaking! Then puts his arm around one of them. Now he's their friend. Suddenly. Says, It's okay now, the sky is gone.

SO-CALLED "SOLUTION" SEGMENT: Later, guests get cured by a "success coach." Offstage. No explanation of how success coach treatment works or who he is, except that he specializes in "phobiology" and has a website. Website of success coach says, *Not hypnosis! Not magic! Click here to order!* Order what? Testimonies of phobics coach has "successfully" treated include:

"Before my treatment I could not even walk past a Gap store without breaking into hives. One time, looking for some mid-rise jeans, I tried to put back the ones on top of the pair I tried on and became very agitated, I couldn't do it. I began to hyperventilate. A salesperson had to bring me a paper bag. I had a very bad sensation of embarrassment. Afterward I would constantly imagine trying to find a pair of jeans or a T-shirt and messing up their piles. I would be obsessed with putting them back as neatly as I found them, but it cannot be done. Later I heard they learn a special folding technique. Well, of course they do. Then I heard about the success coach, and no lie, I went to the Gap the very next day and tried on some jeans and left the pile all mixed up. One pair was on the floor even. I didn't buy anything at all. It was great!"

—Other testimonies of cured phobics with fears of:

Buttons. Boredom. Bolsheviks. Claymation. Two unalike TV shows next to each other on the same videotape. The dollar store. Aldi. The word *supermercado*. Possibly dreaming about naked Quentin Tarantino—to the point where you try to stay awake. Meter maids. People you're not sure why they're famous. Specifically, people on VH1 who comment on stuff from the '80s. Shrink-wrapped gift baskets. American Girl dolls. And rubber gloves. Which could be removed only with more rubber gloves. Which caused phobic a terrible case of dishpan hands.

Which caused phobic to be terribly self-conscious about her hands. Which caused phobic to hide her hands all the time and on dates a lot. Which caused problems because her dates always wanted to hold her hand and then she'd lie about why she didn't want to hold hands with them and then she'd get mixed up in her lies and usually her relationships wouldn't last long, because she was a bad liar. This phobic, in particular, was especially grateful to the success coach for allowing love back into her life after she was cured from her fear of rubber gloves and thus also able to cure her dishpan hands.

—But there are curiously not even vague explanations of the "treatment."

OMNISCIENT NARRATOR again.

• More Qs: When will they get to the part where they explain the nature of phobias? If it's like regular fears? Common fears, fears that make sense, like fear of snakes or public speaking or flying? What about fear that we need? Like the kind that kicks in when you're about to be abducted and suddenly you know what to do even though you never thought about being abducted ever before? Or fear of global warming and so you stop using hairspray or electric can openers or electric anything? What about conceptual fears, like the idea of the Grand Canyon even if you're nowhere near it? Maybe especially if you're nowhere near it. Or: suddenly having zero gravity but not knowing how to propel yourself around so it's no fun. Or: the fear of being wrongly accused of killing someone and then sent to jail. Consider: if you're a perfectly nice person but you're single, or in a long-distance relationship. Maybe: you work at home and you're alone a lot, hence no alibi for the time of the brutal and fatal bludgeoning of the mail carrier (with—a hammer? a brick? what?); he fails to arrive on Saturday, but you know there's mail. Or: the paper delivery guy. Or: the girl with the big tall dog that lives down the street. Girl who, coincidentally, unfortunately, annoys you, and it is known that she annoys you because you've mentioned to a couple of, or several, people about her parking in the spot closest to your house when she's got her very own private garage. Also, she doesn't always pick up after her dog. Really she just annoys you because she's very stylish and thin, wears heels with jeans cuffed all the way up to the knees that you know she saw in *In Style*, her highlighted hair looks good even in a messy little knot on top of her head, drives an SUV, lives in the new condo that blocked out your view of the top part of the skyline. Also: talks to other dog people about how hard it is being a person everyone is intimidated by, especially women, how she has no women friends because their boyfriends all totally want her, because she's a successful (what? does it even matter?), and your best friend and a couple of other friends have also heard about her being so annoying. Then: paper delivery guy delivers the paper with a big headline about the annoying girl. How she's dead. From a bludgeoning. Maybe you gasp and get scared about if you will get bludgeoned. Maybe for half a second you are glad she was bludgeoned. Maybe you feel a little bad about being glad, but not enough. Maybe the cops come around and start asking questions and even though you do not look like anyone who would ever kill anyone on account of you being wholesome (indicated by what—wearing of headbands? modest jeans and T-shirts? your nice face?). Maybe cops go away and come back later and put hand-cuffs on you. Maybe lawyers suggest plea bargaining. Say that you can get a guaranteed max of fifteen years. Maybe you say you can't do that. You aren't guilty. Maybe they say it doesn't matter. Maybe you say it does matter and what about the justice system. Maybe they laugh but then say okay, whatever you want. On trial: testimony of your best friend especially does not help your case because she is very likable and pretty and also unable to lie under oath even for you. Probably she weeps, feeling so bad about it on the stand, which only makes her seem more believ-able plus more sympathetic than you, complainer about neighbors. Plus: your landlord says you've complained about her and they believe him even though he looks like he just smoked a bowl and emptied a forty. Plus: a couple of those kind of people who hang out on the stoop who overheard you complaining to your landlord. Somehow? Also? There's DNA evidence of you on her car. Maybe you made a snowball off it one time. Or: rested your butt on it one time seeing as how it's so big and in your way all the time. Maybe your boyfriend stands by you the whole time and maybe lies and says you were on the phone with him when it happened. Then: you get convicted (for: murder? manslaughter? for how long?) and sent to the state prison. Which is not like the Martha prison where people will be knitting you things. This prison is like *Oz*. But with women. Or like the prisons from TV movies where women gang up on you and try to sodomize you with broomsticks or force you to choose between two equally bad options for whose new girlfriend you get to be, except it isn't even a little bit sexy, your choices are between a fiftyish woman with a frizzy kind of a grayish beehive thing who burned her husband's house down who chain-smoked some seriously hardcore lines onto her face and a younger girl who was maybe cute before the heroin messed up her teeth really bad and who dyes her blond hair black when she can get hold of the dye but who for sure is very very unhealthy. These two choices being like as bad as if they put wigs on two guys from *Prison Break*, not the foxy innocent brothers but the craggy one-handed rapist and maybe the evil guard. And: when you tell them to just choose for you because you think that might make things easier, everyone laughs really hard. In a circle around you. If there were a camera it would go three hundred and sixty degrees to make the viewer feel it more. Long-distance boyfriend breaks up with you. Says: (what? I need space? It's not you, it's me? It's totally you?). That does not seem implausible. Maybe, after you are found guilty and sent away, you go on *20/20* or *48 Hours Mystery* and they act all friendly but then they go, There was DNA evidence of your butt on the SUV, with the tone of like, *I know you did it, bludgeoner*. Maybe you get a lot of letters, letters from men who think bludgeoners are a turn-on, or people who say they believe you're innocent but really don't. Or maybe: you meet a man who seems to sincerely just like you for you and doesn't care, is a very forgiving, nonjudgmental person, and you almost marry him but then when it looks like you might get out of jail he breaks up with you because the whole thing for him is that you're in jail. Then of course you still don't get out of jail. Everything is bad.

More from O.N.: whether something triggers the phobias. How could anyone live like that? No guarantee you won't see a balloon or even an image of a balloon or a clown or whatever on any given day. Seems like it might be easy to just avoid one single thing like balloons, but there's no way to know you won't see a balloon. Do they all just have to stay in? A lot? Balloons and clowns and the sky are sometimes on TV. What do they do inside not watching TV? What about emotional sorts of fear? Abandonment. Failure. Intimacy. Or: all of them. What if you found a long-distance boyfriend *because* of your fear of intimacy? Or: if your long-distance boyfriend breaks up with you and you lose your work-at-home job in the same week, and then a really genuinely nice guy comes along who lives in the same town? And keeps coming by your door with little things you like. Mini-cacti. And says, This made me think of you. Or: he writes you a little zine about a girl who is afraid but the guy keeps coming around with stuff and the drawings are so cute. But still you find something not to like about him, like he's (what?) or (what?) but really it's because he's so close. And you see that he won't go away so you try yelling. And he says, Stop yelling, you're not a yeller. And you try to say mean things like, You're fat, or, My last boyfriend was more man than you'll ever be, but he's onto that too because you have no last boyfriend although the last guy you dated was fat and your new boyfriend knows it. And you try making up more lies like you slept with his brother, or that he is your brother, and he says you're a bad liar and you say, Fine, I'm scared, leave me alone, what do you want? and he says, I want you, and you say that's not one of the choices. And still he stays. So you think about leaving town and changing your identity. Except what if you do that and he finds you? How many times can you do that? What if: all the jail stuff happens, and then you meet this same guy, and he stands by you, and then you do get out of jail because they find the real bludgeoner and your new boyfriend, who wouldn't go away when you were maybe guilty, still won't go away? Then what?

—Last five minutes of talk show:
  • Guests come back out and interns/producers bring back all the things they were afraid of at the beginning of the show.
  • No one is phobic anymore.
  • Clapping.

—What happens after the show?

CLEARVIEW

EVERYTHING IN OUR TOWN WAS NOT ALWAYS CLEAR. But it did take a few years for everyone to realize it always would be from then on.

Maybe I should clarify. (Ha. That's become our little in-town joke.) I don't mean literally everything. Literally most things, but not everything. If a thing somehow contains a thing or covers a thing, it is probably clear. The ground is not clear, but the flowers are, and pretty much anything else that grows out of it. The people of Clearview aren't clear, thank god, nor is anything here invisible. Over time I've come to see that all of this is surprisingly lovely, in a colorless sort of way. You learn to appreciate other things; texture, movement, line. I'm not saying it's convenient.

Clearview used to be your basic, smallish Midwestern city, lots of green but nothing to distinguish it from any other college town, not even the hideous oversized chain hotel that looks as if a spaceship landed in the town square. It had a good school system and my husband was an electrician. Is an electrician. I'm a full-time mom.

The day everything turned clear, I was excited about taking my daughter to her first day of first grade. I had her outfit laid out on her puffy purple chair. We picked it out together: an orange corduroy jumper I embroidered with a pink owl on the front, a green T-shirt underneath, a tiny denim jacket she painted herself on the back, paired with multicolored striped tights and shiny red Mary Janes. My little Astrid loves color. She wants to be a fine artist when she grows up. When she first told me this, I said, *That's wonderful, honey!* and asked her where she heard those words, *fine artist*. It seemed like a sophisticated term I hadn't taught her. She shrugged. She said she didn't think it had to be wonderful, that she'd be happy if it was fine. I didn't explain to her what the term actually meant. I liked her definition better. It augured a sort of satisfaction with herself that artists sometimes don't have, if that's what she ended up doing. It seemed like as good a bet as any—she had some very fresh ideas about art, for a six-year-old. Her entire room was already covered with pictures she'd taped up, anything she liked, some she made, some torn out of magazines or garage-sale books, anything we were willing to let her tear up, and to me it was as bright, bold, and interesting to look at as any collage I've seen in a museum. She called them her dreamers.

That morning, it looked like someone had taped up—well, not cellophane exactly, but try to imagine a sort of textured vellum. My baby's flamboyant outfit seemed to be made of clear vinyl, with the ridges you'd find in corduroy, but none of the color. The owl I embroidered was there, but now appeared in what seemed to be clear thread. Astrid woke up before we did and ran into our room crying, *My colors, my colors are gone! My dreamers!*

Groggy, we of course thought she was having a bad dream, talking nonsense. Jake rubbed the sleep out of his eyes first, shook me. *Whoa*, he said.

C'mere, honey. I pulled Astrid into bed with us. I looked around. I took in clear doors, clear walls, clear blankets. *This is someone's bad dream. Let's go back to sleep.* We all closed our eyes, but no one went back to sleep. We assumed it was just us until Jake got up to look out the window. Our whole neighborhood was clear, although the streets were empty. We stayed in bed for a while. We had no idea what else to do. *Why would god do this, Mommy?* Astrid asked me. I told her I wasn't one hundred percent sure god was responsible, but that if he was, he must have had a good reason. *He?* Astrid said, kind of annoyed. *Not he*, she admonished us. *Okay, she? It?* I said, to which she shook her head and said, *No, Mommy, not she, not it,* and left it at that, knowing we wouldn't get it.

Astrid more or less came out of the womb believing in god. Jake was half-Jewish—emphasis on the half—and I had only a vague notion that there was something greater than myself, although I certainly didn't think there was anyone up there performing large-scale puppetry. But Astrid believed, and we let her, and her beliefs were all her own. If you pinned me down, I'd say she most closely resembled a Buddhist, if Buddha is not a he, she, or it and has a dog named Smarty.

We turned on our clear TV to check the local news. The field reporters looked horrified standing outside in their clear suits. Whatever journalistic distance they were supposed to maintain was offset by their startled, uncomfortable expressions. Plus, they didn't know anything more than we did. They were just like, *As you can see, everything in town has suddenly become transparent. There's speculation that it may be a weather issue. As of now there are no reports of similar occurrences in other cities. There are no reports of casualties. The mayor is planning a press conference by phone later today. We'll bring you more as soon as we have it. Back to you, Marlon.*

From our house, Jake saw other people at their windows looking equally confused. It seemed like everyone had to be thinking the same thing. It's hard to know how to begin dealing with a problem when putting on your clothes to go investigate still leaves you as good as naked. Jake, who'd always been the kind of guy who could care less what you saw of him, volunteered to go next door and see if anyone knew what was going on. When he rang the bell, his neighbor and good friend Arnie hid behind the door, which of course hid nothing. *What do you think we should do?* Jake asked him. Arnie said he was going to crack open a six-pack and stay in until it changed back or he didn't care.

The mayor, as we all know now, blamed it on the federal government. Much as I love to blame just about anything on the government, it was hard to make that connection, and like most folks, we could have cared less why it happened, we just wanted our color back.

Eventually the matter was declared a disaster and directed to FEMA. A FEMA rep took one circle around town in a helicopter from a safe height, of course, heaven forbid he got caught with see-through pants, and proposals were made for relocation. The mayor also proposed that in the meantime we try to proceed as usual, that keeping businesses open was critical to the economy. He tried to tell us that if everyone was clear we were all on an equal playing field. The population that was heavily invested in miracle bras found this amusing, considering it took him all of a day to put together the Clearview version of a Popemobile, which amounted to him surrounding himself with as many body-guards as he needed to hide his flesh. The mayor promised the city would provide free counseling to anyone who wanted it.

FEMA, at this time, was unaware that relocation wasn't a perfect solution. Some people tried to leave town immediately, only to find that their personal effects remained clear in other towns. Others left town and led normal, opaque lives in other cities. There seemed to be no one thing that those lucky people had in common in terms of who'd turn out to be opaque some-where else and who wouldn't. Speculation was there might be a freaky gene of some kind, but no one came rushing to town to discover it. For our part, we didn't really know what to do.

Unlike Jake, I'm pretty modest. I made a stab at getting dressed by putting on as many clear sweaters and jeans as would render my near-nakedness sort of nebulously fuzzy, but I couldn't bear the thought of sending Astrid to school that way.

Like I said, we all thought it would change back at first, and so a lot of us stayed in for a while. It seemed better than going out. Anyone who could work from home did, even though home for a lot of people was apartments where you could see through into the floors above and below and next door. We lived in a house that was at least set back off the street and slightly away from the houses around us. Trees and hedges were little protection for anyone. They were clear as well. There was nothing to hide behind, or at least that's what we thought.

Certain kinds of crimes went way down, as you might imagine. If you can't really conceal a weapon, or you know, *yourself*, you kinda lose the element of surprise. Marriages fell apart when husbands and wives quickly discovered evidence of affairs, compulsive shopping, pot stashes hidden in the backs of drawers. Alcohol and substance abuse went up. People were lonely. Just not lonely enough to go out.

Jake went to work right away. He really didn't care. I think a little part of him even liked it. I homeschooled Astrid and she did not like it. She was a social creature who lived to meet new people, and although she, like many people, tried to maintain and cultivate friendships by phone and online, of the three of us, she felt the isolation most keenly. I'd always been a homebody, and it almost wouldn't have made that much difference to me, but Astrid suffered.

We knew right away that moving wasn't an option. One trip to the mall in the next town over established that Jake and I took our clear clothes with us. Astrid, however, got her colors back right at the edge of town and could not conceal her joy. So we considered our options:

1) Move to another town so Astrid could thrive, and be semi-naked parents, always.

2) Send Astrid to boarding school.

This, for us, was like a real-life game of *What's Better*, where you think of two things and you get to keep one and the other has to be banished from the face of the earth. Sending Astrid to boarding school seemed as good as banishing her from the face of the earth as far as I was concerned, but moving somewhere with her only to embarrass her on a daily basis with essentially nude parents didn't seem much better. We asked her what she thought. She swore she didn't care, but I felt sure she had no idea what she was in for.

She did not want to leave us, but she was obviously depressed without color. Other people were medicating their children, and I can't say we didn't think about it for a minute, but I didn't want to medicate her for reacting to a highly weird situation, you know, appropriately. We tried to convince her that we would be fine if she decided to go and we'd visit her and she'd visit us as much as possible, and we almost packed her off. Even thinking about it was, frankly, awful for all of us. She's our only child. She stopped eating much of anything for about a week while we talked about it. So we we came up with a third option—stay in Clearview and be a semi-naked family.

People eventually wandered out, myself included, but we did not become more free. People cultivated denial. We all looked away from other people's bodies, but we didn't look into their eyes either. We stopped hugging altogether. If we bumped into people at the store or wherever, our conversations were often reduced to mere syllables, our gazes flitting about so as not to land anywhere on an actual person. *Hey. Hey. You good? Good. You? Good. Jake? Yah, good. Kids? Good. Work? Good, good. 'Kay, good. 'Kay, bye.*

Three FEMA directors came and went, but they weren't really to blame. They were ridiculously slow to throw any money in our town's direction, but even when they finally did, they tried a lot of different things and nothing worked. Scientists were consulted. Theories were posited. Anything that came into town in color became clear. If you could leave, you did. If you couldn't, you dealt with it however you could. The population decreased by about half.

Astrid was so happy not to be going away that she decided to make the best of it. She said she would go to school right here. I told her that only maybe five kids were going to school anymore. She said, *Well, now there will be six.*

We underestimated her. Astrid went to school and did what no grown-ups had been able to do since the whole thing happened. She was not used to people not looking at each other. When she would raise her hand in class, she wouldn't get called on, because the teachers wouldn't look at her or anyone else. She would shout, *Hey!* if she wanted to answer. One day she couldn't take it anymore, and she came up with what I thought was a genius idea. For show-and-tell, she was going to show herself. We asked her if she was sure she wanted to do that. *I'm sure*, she said.

Astrid went to school and when it was her turn, stood in front of the class. Her teacher asked her what she brought to talk about. She said, *I brought myself. I am a six-year-old girl from Clearview. I have brown hair and green eyes with a little tiny bit of gold.* Astrid's teacher and two classmates were somewhat confused. *Look at me*, Astrid said. At first no one did. *Look at me*! she insisted.

You're half-naked, said one boy.

Duh, so are you, Astrid said. *And god is all the way naked.*

No he isn't, he wears sandals and a dress.

So you say, said Astrid. Her teacher tried to direct her to her seat with a shooing motion. *But I'm not done.*

Yes, her teacher said, *you are.*

No, said Astrid, *I'm not*. She was promptly sent to the principal's office.

Why do you think you're here, Astrid? the principal asked, focusing on a ball of clear rubber bands.

Because no one will look at me when I'm talking. Like you.

This is how it is now, Astrid. We don't want anyone to feel uncomfortable.

But I don't feel uncomfortable.

Well, you should.

Astrid was sent home that day with a note from the principal stating that the only reason she didn't get detention was because they had no one available to supervise things like detention. As it was, her class, the only one in her school, was made up of one kindergartner, two second graders, one fourth grader, one sixth grader, and a toddler they were essentially just babysitting because he had nowhere else to go. The daycare centers were all closed.

No way was this going to fly with me or Jake. We went to see the principal and defended our child, but it was for naught. We were back to evil *What's Better*, but then Jake added the suggestion that we move to a nudist colony somewhere. I thought that seemed extreme. We went back to homeschooling. I asked Astrid how she'd make her art without color. *Maybe I'll work in shapes,* she said. I admired her willingness.

I was feeling worse than hopeless. I felt resigned. Astrid wasn't having it. *Let's go to church*, she said at around four on a Thursday afternoon. We'd never been to church, ever. I tried to explain that church services were mostly on Sunday. *That doesn't make any sense*, she said. *Let's go anyway and see what happens.* We asked her if she had one in mind. *Doesn't matter*, she said. *God will meet us there.*

This was when I realized my kid might be onto something.

We walked over to a church that was two blocks down from us. No one was there but a janitor and a woman praying in front of a row of candles. *We'd like to speak to god, please,* Astrid said to the janitor.

Yeah, you and me both, he said, mopping. Astrid looked at me. She wasn't quite old enough to perceive sarcasm.

How about if we just light a candle and pray, honey? Astrid liked candles. We lit three.

One for god and one for Smarty and one for Clearview, our daughter said. We kneeled down next to the woman who was praying silently.

What's up, goddy? Astrid said. *I know you have a plan but people are kinda weirding out down here. I've been doing my best, but I miss color and plus no one looks at me is the worst thing. You have to look at a kid.*

God, I said, *I would ask that if this is part of your plan, to help us understand it somehow.*

Yeah, like with a sign! Astrid said. *Like the time you sent the puddle with your and Smarty's picture in it the day you had on those fuzzy hats. That was so funny.*

This was the first we'd heard of this. Jake and I looked at each other and shrugged, sort of giggling. I wondered if the lady next to us was listening. For sure she wasn't looking.

Check you later, god, Astrid said. *Okay, guys, let's go look for signs now!*

This is around the time where we started reconsidering medication. Astrid got a little obsessed with looking for signs. Meanwhile, the population dwindled even further and Clearview threatened to become a ghost town. I swear I saw a tumbleweed roll past the spaceship hotel. Astrid, of course, saw it too, and although it turned out to be a beach ball, which was still weird, she took it as just one of her many signs. *Maybe we're supposed to move to the beach!* Anything and everything became a possible sign. Signs became signs.

And on the subject of literal signs, after the city quickly blew through all available funds on failed solutions, the townspeople started doing what they could. It was discovered that duct tape worked well to cover things like street signs so that they could be read, but even so, people drove very carefully when they drove at all, because you could barely see the lines on the pavement. Anyone who stayed found more and more ways to adapt. Anything that was previously color-coded fell by the wayside; things like national terror alerts meant nothing to us, and it seemed obvious that a lot of people would sooner die alone inside their homes than evacuate naked. Distinct but simple shapes became a common way of identifying basic things; a bread shape meant food, a heart shape signified a hospital, a drip shape meant water, a five-sided house shape was, you know, a house.

None of this, however, helped the problem of people not looking at each other. People connected almost exclusively at a distance. E-mail and text messaging became more popular than ever, but it fostered a false sort of intimacy that often ensues when people aren't face to face, where from the safety of your own home you can tell someone any and every last detail of your life, when in reality, or IRL as they say, romances that seemed to bloom online would almost invariably wilt when the couple met in person, only to engage in a disappointed fleeting glance before looking away. If they lasted longer than a cocktail date, the real-life behavior surrounding dating had become almost impossible to accept. People went to greater lengths to keep their secrets, to hold on to anything resembling privacy, and it resulted in things like an absurd number of people going all the way to the gym just to use the bathroom so as not to embarrass themselves around anyone they might not care to share such intimacies with, which resulted in people eating and drinking less so they wouldn't have to make so many trips to the gym, and this is just one thing. Some people went to the gym to floss. There was, naturally, a small contingent of people who were comfortable enough with themselves before this happened that in a way it sort of empowered them when it did come to pass. I wasn't quite in that category, although Jake and Astrid were. I was never overweight or anything, but I wasn't much one for the gym either. I knew I looked really really good, in clothes.

Astrid came closest to making us believe in her signs when she made a discovery during an effort to build a playhouse out of a refrigerator box. It was surprising that no one had discovered it before, because believe me, everyone in town had tried to make clothing out of any unlikely thing you could think of that might possibly stay opaque in front of the skin: hair, paint, bird feathers. One guy tried to stuff a suit lining with live bees. When she got inside, Astrid's clear cardboard house completely obscured her body, taking on the typical brown color of cardboard, and to her total thrill, retained the colors she had painted upon it.

So yeah, clothing made out of corrugated cardboard—not exactly built for comfort. But it got people out of the house and optimistic again. More kids went back to school, more people went to work, business got a little better. It didn't do much to bring the people back who didn't have to be there. The town was still, by all accounts, depressed. But life went on as normally as it could in a place where you could see through just about everything. Once in a while there'd be an article in the *New York Times* or some national magazine about life in our quirky little burg: Look at the plucky people, dressed in cardboard! More than once, some asshole pundit suggested that we brought it on ourselves for living in a town called Clearview in the first place, like it was inevitable that this would happen, that other people in cities called Clearview should get out while they could. Granted, maybe it made as much sense as any other theory, but come on. We live in enough fear as it is. This is what I hear when pundits talk about us: Maybemaybemaybe. Muh muh muh muh. Maybe.

Muh muh. Maybe. Maybemaybemaybe. Maybe *whatever*. Our Clearview was odd, but worse things happen.

The artists, as they will, knew a good thing when they saw it. Rent and real estate was cheap, cheaper than it had been before this all went down and it was pretty cheap then. The additional price of cardboard clothing seemed a small one. They came and made art and opened galleries in empty gas stations and opened coffeehouses in other empty places like the empty bus depot and the empty sporting goods store and opened cardboard clothing stores in empty clothing stores, sometimes rent-free because no trace of the original owners remained. More articles in national papers followed. We got a little tourism. The spaceship hotel hired thirty new people. People wanted a glimpse of our unique way of life, like we were the Amish.

Astrid spotted something again. *Look, Mommy, a new sign!* We never argued with her, but to be honest we never really saw what she saw. This time she was pointing to a large sign in the shape of a grande foam latte. It was in front of a new coffee bar that was about to open, one of the big national chains. We hadn't even had one of those before the town went clear. A few days after that we got a Whole Foods.

You can probably guess the rest of the story.

WHAT OUR WEEK WAS LIKE

WE STARTED ON THURSDAYS. Thursdays at Shorty's drinks were a dollar so we drank as many as we could. We squeezed past townies on Thursdays, we yelled over the noise and we ate popcorn on Thursdays and we listened to The Doors on Thursdays and we drank. We drank mostly beer unless we didn't like beer and we drank anything sweet and we ordered our next drink before we finished the last. We noticed cute juniors on Thursdays and butted our eyelashes for cocktails and it worked and on Thursdays we thought sarcasm was funny. On Thursdays we kept the buzz going. On Thursdays we drank because we were legal, we drank because we were young and because it was almost Friday and we drank until it was Friday. We drank on Fridays wherever. On Fridays we heard there were cute juniors at a dorm party but there weren't so we drank. On Fridays we drank in our rooms, down the hall, in the hall, in the lounge, on the eighth floor, on the ninth floor, at the stoner bar before it burned down, at preppy bars and frat parties, and we drank at parties off campus where someone knew someone who roomed with someone who knew us somehow. We told everyone and anyone we liked cute juniors. We told stoned preppy frat boys we didn't know that we liked cute juniors. On Fridays at midnight, stoned, we went to see *The Kentucky Fried Movie* or *The Rocky Horror Picture Show* and we shouted, "Dammit, Janet," at both movies even though you were only supposed to shout it at one. On Fridays, drunk and stoned, *The Kentucky Fried Movie* was hilarious and so were we. On Fridays, drunk and stoned, everything was hilarious until we forgot where we parked the car and life was not worth living. We left our coats at the stoner bar or the preppy bar or the frat party or the midnight movie, we stumbled back to our dorms, freezing and lost and drunk, we lay down on our beds just for a minute before we changed, on Saturdays we woke up in our clothes but we never used the phrase "passed out." On Saturdays we forgot stuff. On Saturdays we said to each other, "We were so WASTED last night, it was AWESOME!" even though we couldn't remember half of it. We heard cute juniors were going to The Barge, for sure, on Saturdays. We took disco naps on Saturdays and we drank at The Barge, which was not really a barge, really it was a gay disco on the edge of town. We went shopping on Saturdays with money we didn't have to buy new outfits or at least a new accessory because we never wore the same exact outfit to The Barge twice, and on Saturday nights we got dressed up to go drink at The Barge and disco dance in our new accessories in front of semi-pornographic gay slides. We drank while waiting in line for The Barge, we drank while cutting the line for The Barge, we drank while we waited for the right song at The Barge, a song that wasn't "beat," and then we rushed the dance floor, drunkish, when the DJ finally played Sylvester. (*Youuu maake me feeel . . . Mi-ighty reeeeeeal!*) Saturdays we ate frozen Milky Way bars at The Barge, drunk, we flirted with everyone on Saturdays, drunk, we wanted everyone to love us, drunk, we made out at The Barge, drunk, sometimes with whoever, sometimes with cute juniors, sometimes on the dance floor, sometimes in the ladies' room, sometimes right after making out with cute juniors in the ladies' room when we saw them hitting on skanky sophomore transfers with their butts hanging out of their white pleather minis, we made out with whoever on Saturdays, preferably situated close enough to cute juniors so that jealousy could ensue, but far enough so that it seemed accidental. Jealousy never ensued, and it never seemed accidental, but this was nothing one more Slow Comfortable Screw couldn't fix. We thought saying Slow Comfortable Screw, especially to a cute bartender, was very funny and sexy, drunk. We thought adding Up against the Wall to the end of Slow Comfortable Screw would seal the deal, drunk. On Saturdays we never left The Barge sober, we never left before the lights came on, before last dance, last chance for romance. We drove home, drunk, with someone, sometimes even cute juniors. We knew their first names, we knew who their friends were, we knew what we were doing, we said to ourselves, we knew we wanted something different, sober. Saturdays we tried to sleep on someone's dirty black sheets, less drunk. Saturdays we didn't care, Sundays we regretted it. Never the drinking, not the drinking and the driving combination, only the driving home with someone, only the someone we woke up with, only the someone we woke up with whose roommates were all grinning with the promise of forth-coming gossip and horrible nicknames relating to various possible acts performed the night before, drunk. Sundays the someone who wouldn't drive us to our home even though they didn't seem to want us so much at their home anymore, forced us to wait for a ride with a soon-to-be-gossiping roommate until a football game was over or take the bus in our rumpled outfits from the night before, knowing that people on the bus would recognize our Saturday night outfits on Sunday morning and shake their heads, possibly. Sundays waiting for a ride we drank bitter coffee made with paper towel filters at someone and his roommate's apartment, hung over. Sundays there were also paper towels acting as toilet paper at someone and his roommate's apartment (if we were so lucky that there was anything acting as toilet paper at all). Sundays in someone's bathroom we didn't dare look at anything for fear of extreme uncleanliness, especially ourselves in the mirror. Sundays we slept, woke up for a sandwich delivery or to put quarters in machines for cheese crackers or microwave pancakes, watched something on TV, and went back to sleep. We never drank on Sundays, unless there was a barbecue or a Super Bowl party or an Oscar party or a dorm party or unless we knew we were going to fail the astro test anyway or unless someone had some. Mondays we ate baked potatoes or frozen yogurt in the cafeteria and called it lunch and we gossiped about who drove home with someone and if the gossip was about us we tried to do damage control. We said we didn't really like cute juniors after all, even though we still did, in spite of everything. On Mondays we told tales out of school. We said cute juniors weren't all that in the bedroom, even though we couldn't really remember if they were or weren't. Even though we ourselves were for sure not all that in the bedroom, seeing as how we had no previous experience in the bedroom. For a while we didn't drink on Mondays but then we did. Monday night was the night. We went to Shorty's and drank and ate popcorn and played Name That Tune and it was always The Doors even when it wasn't and this was hilarious. Tuesdays we skipped class and smoked some pot but only if someone had some. Sometimes on Tuesdays we smoked pot from bongs or little pipes on the ninth floor, the druggy floor, sometimes they were ceramic, sometimes they were wood, sometimes they were tall, sometimes they smelled really bad, sometimes we didn't care. On Tuesdays pot was never bought, by anyone, anywhere, any day, as far as we knew, and we watched TV stoned and thought it was hilarious until we saw four Kristy McNichols and freaked out. We almost never drank on Tuesdays until we did. Later our roommate who had a midterm yelled at us which brought us so down. On Tuesdays we made drama where there was none. We stormed out on Tuesdays and went to the lounge to look for someone to feel sorry for us, became best buds with the Iranian students who were actually studying who we never talked to before who understood where we were coming from and we hijacked them to Shorty's, stoned, so we could drink. On Tuesdays we paid full price for drinks at Shorty's and we ran into cute juniors and gave them a piece of our mind. Cute juniors told us we were so cute when we were mad and we got more mad and made cute juniors buy us drinks. On Tuesdays we teased cute juniors and made them go home alone. Wednesdays we went to class but slept through it or passed notes about weird transfer students or mean roommates or who we left The Barge with and what were we going to wear to The Barge this week-end. We almost never drank on Wednesdays until we did. We almost never went home with cute juniors unless we did. We went home over and over, not meaning to, with cute juniors we crushed on so hard for so long who would never feel the same until years later when they thought they might feel marginally the same and came to visit us after college but in the cold hard light of New York City we realized that big sleepy green eyes weren't really a character trait we could build a relationship on and that our judgment about these things was maybe weak at best. That pot wasn't something people had in common. We were almost never hungover until we were, we almost never threw up until we did. We almost never took pills until we did. We almost never mixed pills and alcohol until we did. We tried to pace ourselves, which means to drink a lot slowly but steadily as opposed to drinking a lot like a chain-smoker, which worked when we were eighteen but not when we were twenty. We did this for four and a half years until we graduated and we used the word *party* as a verb without irony. Sometimes we waited for the weekend, often we didn't wait for the weekend, after that we mixed it up for several more years until we looked around and saw that it was not so much we anymore as it was just one of us.

THE GLISTENING HEAD OF RICKY RICARDO BEGS FURTHER EXPERIMENTATION

I WAS HARDLY SURPRISED WHEN the 13" I bought used twenty years ago finally gave out. The picture had been breaking up into weird lines for a while and then one day I turned it on and got nothing. So I did something I'd never done before: I bought a new TV. You have to understand that most of the stuff in my house once belonged to someone else, and that it's mine now for reasons both financial and sentimental. Not TVs so much as some of the furniture, like the red desk that used to have a matching trundle bed I slept in from fifth to ninth grade, a set of Victorian chairs that are seriously uncomfortable and way too short for the table (were people shorter then or what?), and a little black hutch that was on the porch when I moved in. I've never had a ton of extra cash, although there have been occasional windfalls, but even when that happens, usually I'll spend the money on something practical, like nice sheets or towels, or going to the dentist. I'd love to buy a new couch, but I've never been able to bring myself to do it. Something about guilt. Plus it seems like a commitment. Red velvet appeals to me now, but what if it seems Vegas-loungey in five years?

TV's a no-brainer. I can go a few hours without it, I can go to work, that sort of thing, but a day without TV? What kind of life is that? Why would anyone do that to themselves? So I marched right out and got myself a new 13" for $79.99, which is exactly a penny less than I paid my college roommate's cousin all those years ago for the used one that just died. I felt grown-up. Plus the new fall season had just started.

Imagine my disappointment, though, to find that the TV had a serious defect in that the top of it was loose, almost like it was a lid, except why would you need a lid for your TV? You don't keep things in there. It was about time for *Caleb's Little Sexy Town* to start and I had no time to rush back out to the store, so I plugged it in figuring I'd make an exchange the next day. Except the lid wouldn't stay on tight, so there I was jiggling that lid around, and when I looked down into the chassis I can assure you I did not expect to see a 9" Caleb himself walking around in there. For a second I thought he was some kind of promotional action figure or something, because not only was he incredibly lifelike, he was looking up at me, trying not to break out of his scene and gesturing with his head like I ought to put the lid back on. But come on! What would you do if you had a 9" live-action Caleb inside your TV? Of course I took him out! He wasn't very nice about it, really. *What are you doing?* he said. *You have to put me back.* I didn't want to be rude, but he was 9" high. I had the obvious advantage. I said, *Come on, Caleb, lighten up! What's the rush?* He got all huffy like I shouldn't have called him Caleb and said, *You can't take people out of the TV like that.* I said, *Well, I think I can!* But to be honest, he was so cranky, and I thought, well, of all the people on TV, maybe there's a better choice. So I put him back, and he didn't thank me, you can be sure. I told him he was lucky I didn't put him in a dress.

I switched channels and same thing every time, a tiny live show in my TV. Naturally, when I landed on a Lucy rerun and saw the glistening head of Ricky Ricardo reflecting up at me, I couldn't resist, but he quickly melted into a gooey little black-and-white puddle that ended up being kind of hard to get off the floor. (I concluded only after pulling out Ed Sullivan and Jackie Gleason that dead black-and-white people don't keep for long outside of the TV, but that if you let the puddles dry first, they come right up.) So I stuck with shows from the last thirty or forty years where I was pretty sure everyone was still living. I realized I had a golden opportunity to improve on some shows I thought could use some help and set about the task of recasting as well as entirely reworking a few in particular. I decided quickly that as tempting as it was, I had a moral obligation not to get involved with news or politics, in spite of my addiction to cable news and my incessant hope that the so-called Reign of Horror might someday end and during which time I briefly developed a painful, inexplicable, and of course deeply shameful—not to mention severely age-inappropriate—crush on Donald Rumsfeld. I know. He was, like, a hundred. Mostly it was just aesthetic—I always turn the volume down on politicians anyway—but partly it was because I'd heard he ran into the Pentagon on September 11 and rescued people and shit and I mean, that's pretty hot. I got over it.

Anyway, I gave some consideration to scooping up some particularly heinous people and putting them in an episode of *Milt the Goat Dog* or something, but you know, I'm not god, and maybe I don't know what's best in that area. Admittedly I came to this conclusion only after I tried working with videotape because there were certain historical events I had a mind to set right. But it turns out that even though it looks the same, when you reach down into a taped show, what comes out is a type of bubble solution that tends to be extremely hot, which I discovered the hard way after grabbing a fistful of Nazis out of a PBS documentary.

I distributed several particularly annoying bow-tied pundits into a selection of Spanish-language serials (a number of passionate long-term affairs came out of this in spite of the language barrier). I switched band members from different episodes of *Way behind the Music*, which unsurprisingly didn't change much—some of them didn't even notice—and also I had a ton of fun changing people's clothes, especially on the entertainment shows. Celebrities get very cranky about this, even if they've been known for their fashion crimes and you've put them in someone's tasteful Armani.

Most of these changes resulted in spectacular ratings and a few marriages, which was when I realized I had a gift. The special TV had clearly been sent to me for the greater purposes of drawing people closer and bringing others together who might otherwise never have met. I came to consider this service work.

In the process of improving things, it occurred to me that I had overlooked another obvious benefit: sex. I'd need to figure a way around the 9" problem, but in the meantime I made a nice place in my underwear drawer for Brad Brad-Brad from *Sexy Doctors Sex It Up*, who didn't waste any time commenting on the contents of the drawer. *Nice*, he said, leaning on a satin b-cup. *I see some of these still have the tags on*, he said, struggling to hoist the bra onto his shoulder so he could show me the tag. He didn't bark as much as Caleb but he did try to escape at one point, and I was glad to catch him by the door so I could point out the sparkly residue of the Valderrama twins, who managed to get the door open only to turn immediately into a pile of glitter on the doormat. (I vacuumed them up hoping they'd somehow reconstitute themselves, but the ensuing noise I heard coming from the vacuum turned out to be Harry Letterman, who got loose while I wasn't looking, saying he just needed a little alone time. BTW, I wasn't trying to have sex with the Valderramas— not that there's anything wrong with that—but I just wasn't. I was trying to talk the skinny one into eating part of my donut.) Brad Brad, it turns out, was attracted to me but had concerns about the size difference, which motivated me to figure a way to hook the 13" up to the 27" in the living room, which worked after some playing around with cable wires and VCRs, but think about it. I couldn't afford one of those giant 6' screens but Brad needed to be big, so I threw those Victorian chairs into my rusty wagon and checked out a few pawn shops before I finally found one that both had a giant TV and would take the chairs, and as soon as I got home I pried the top of that thing open in a big hurry. I waited for the right moment and shoved Nurse Doris into a utility closet and Brad-Brad climbed out all on his own and it was good. He swore he'd come back whenever I wanted if I let him return to work, and he did.

But I started liking him, which for me rarely results in anything pleasant even with fully-sized men, plus at first I couldn't get into the TV at all. For the most part I didn't really want to. I liked it fine on my side of the TV, but we did end up trying, because at that point I was looking at it like you would a long-distance relationship: at some point someone has to move. Plus I kind of wanted to do it somewhere in the hospital, which he was as usual amenable to, though as soon as I hoisted my leg over the side of the big-screen, I could feel it becoming sort of rubbery, flexible in a way that a leg shouldn't be flexible, and I was afraid of meeting a reverse Ricky Ricardo kind of fate, which in a way would be even worse because it'd have been on a highly rated television show, which is not the way anyone really wants to become famous, so I jumped right back out. I threw a few things down in there that I didn't need, to see what would happen to them, and it turns out that the flexibility was just a brief transitional stage. The funny thing was, every time I put something in there, they acted like it was just meant to be there, like Dr. Oswald would just walk down the hall and pick up my old sneaker and go, *Damn junkies.*

Anyway, that was around the time I started to see Brad Brad-Brad's picture in the tabloids with various twenty-year-old starlets, and I'd be lying if I told you it didn't cross my mind to turn them into glitter, but that had been an accident, and I wasn't looking to hurt anyone. So rather than put myself through the inevitable defeat of being compared to anyone who might pose in their panties on the cover of a magazine (which is an alarming lot of people), I turned my attentions toward the one I've loved the most all along: Rocket Dude del Toro. He had recently split up with his longtime love Australia Wilson-Phoenix after they appeared on a reality show in which celebrities reenact scenes from congressional hearings. Australia I guess got in touch with her inner right-winger and Rocket, who always had lefty political aspirations, could no longer reconcile their differences. I think it's obvious I had something to offer him, because how in the hell are you going to run for office if you're 9" tall?

I yanked him right out of a dreary fake filibuster about hybrid hovercrafts for which he thanked me immensely. I gave him a different drawer than Brad's, figuring I could squash any desire that might arise about leaving if he were sleeping in a cashmere bed, plus of course I didn't want him to develop any negative associations by comparing himself to my former flame, and I thought it best to wait on the romance anyway, since there were bigger things at stake. I knew I never had a chance at running for office myself, since I had no acting resume whatsoever, but I had romantic notions about being the Hillary to his tiny Bill. (But not the Bill to his tiny Hillary. That would just be weird.)

Unfortunately, I was unable to "supersize" him (his joke), which would seem an obvious disadvantage in the political arena. Rocket, being who he was, turned this into a platform for minority rights, particularly the tiny and invisible. (Invisibility had become a serious problem in the last few years; scientists had developed an allergy-free peanut, but invisibility was an unexpected side effect.) I carried Rocket to the streets with a megaphone and his message was heard. He grew immensely popular, organizing voter registration campaigns that garnered thousands of new voters, and went on to run successfully for Congress, where he championed arts funding and universal health care and was the swing vote in finally bringing the troops home from the thirty-year war in Iraq.

I tried many ways and many times to enlarge him. We'd long since fallen in love, but attempts at lovemaking were awkward at first. You simply cannot French kiss a man whose mouth is a centimeter wide without risk of asphyxiation. If, however, you place one in just the right spot in your pants, you can experience something truly transcendent. Sadly, I could not offer him much in this area; you can imagine my clumsy efforts without my spelling it out. Such is my selfless little Rocket, though, he loves me anyway and doesn't seem to care. I became Mrs. Rocket Dude del Toro in September of last year, and we are expecting our first child next winter. We don't know whether it will be big or small, invisible or shaped like a TV, but we have a name picked out either way. We're going to call it Yes!

DONOVAN'S CLOSET

WHAT I'M ABOUT TO TELL you notwithstanding, I am not a stalker. Or a boyfriend-stealer. I ended up in Donovan's closet entirely by accident.

We'd been flirting for a while. He used to be in a band with my friend Jason, who was now in this band Diatribe. I was never really much into the music scene before that (I love music, but the whole indie music scene eluded me—something to do with a degree of coolness I found intimidating; as Jason once said, "You could weave a tapestry from the mutton chops alone"), but I started going to all Jason's shows, to show my support, and so did Donovan. It was easy to see why they were friends—they both had that brainy rock star thing going on, which for Jason equaled a $50 non-haircut haircut, Levi's, and the occasional designer jacket (he had a high-paying day gig writing commercial jingles), and on Donovan, the 29-year-old prematurely balding shaved head, black-rimmed glasses (nerd cool), and lab coat.

Donovan's getting a degree in chemistry. He's a chemist. He's a chemist who plays in a band. (His band is called U.) You have to admit that's pretty cool. He plays drums. Possibly you already know that there are all kinds of drummer jokes (I didn't), that the drummer is typically seen as the slacker of the band, but I *love* drums, and the chemist-drummer combo was a total indie rock do as far as I was concerned. (I know thing zero about chemistry, which in some weird way made him even more appealing. I felt like his understanding of chemistry, even if I was unable to ever converse with him on the subject, just put him on this other level of intelligence. I felt like only grown-ups knew about chemistry. I didn't even know anyone who'd taken it in high school.) Plus, Donovan! Who doesn't need a boyfriend named Donovan?

Jason and I initially became friends primarily on the basis of our mutual love of shopping. (It was some time later that I found out he's actually kind of a brilliant and a crazy over-achiever who paints and writes novels in his spare time.) You have to appreciate a straight guy who loves to shop but avoids that whole tucked-in, primpy, hair gel look that there's a serious infestation of over at those bars on Rush Street. Jason can wear a thousand-dollar jacket in such a way that you notice Jason before you notice the jacket. Which we agree to be one of the prime fashion directives—1) If someone says you look great and then an hour goes by before they say anything about the jacket, you have made a successful purchase. If that same jacket can go entirely unnoticed at the hipster bars, then you have a gift. 2) The right pair of boots can make many things possible. 3) Labels go on the inside.

I'm fairly certain he goes shopping more than I do. We've gotten into a thing where we call each other from our cells regarding new purchases. (Or regarding perfect future spouses spotted while shopping, like the woman he followed into Agnes B. or the cute but bitter hipster I saw picking through boys T-shirts at Village Thrift who'd overheard me mocking his quest for perfect irony and didn't seem to appreciate it.)

Anyway, Jason introduced me to Donovan at one of their shows, although I can't say I was immediately rocketed into a fourth dimension of attraction. (Most of the people I've been wildly attracted to [e.g., Cute Bitter Hipster] have turned out to be men of lesser ambition. To whom the oft-cited mantra "selling out" expands to include concepts like *paying rent, having car insurance*, and sometimes even *having a phone*. All of which, when spoken aloud, must be heavily italicized. I prided myself on my ironic detachment too, when I was seventeen. I'm thirty now.) But Donovan was obviously really funny and really smart, and, entirely unsolicited, mentioned that he loved two of my favorite authors, and after just a few minutes of gabbing I was sure that he really was going to be my new boyfriend. Sometimes you can just tell. And every time I saw him it was the same thing, we'd just gab and it would be obvious that we could keep gabbing but then he'd never ask me out. I consulted my *Magic 8 Ball* key ring, which I only used in emergencies for two reasons: because there was always a chance I wouldn't get the answer I wanted (it had an uncanny rate of accuracy; I know, but whatever), and because nine times out of ten it landed on the line between two answers, and you could never get it to stick on one or the other before it picked two more—my solution to this was always to choose whichever one my eye landed on first, but sometimes the mind plays tricks this way (always in my favor). In this instance, when I asked if Donovan was going to be my new boyfriend, it landed on one very nebulous answer: *Can't tell.* For the moment I decided it was best to leave that alone.

I fantasized about him for weeks. In my fantasies, there's sex, of course, which is needless to say brilliant (so brilliant that I can almost pretend there are no appliances involved), but mostly he naps with me on the couch (I have a bigger couch, in my fantasies) and we do the crossword puzzle in our pajamas (he wears pajamas!) and we have a word-of-the-day from the *Oxford English Dictionary* (you have to pick a random word and use it in a sentence) and we listen to *All Things Considered* and he explains to me whatever I don't understand but not in a condescending way and he reads to me—he reads to me—he reads me to sleep and we watch Adam Sandler movies (indicating our well-balanced cultural palate) and he never says anything mean, he only says nice things, really smart nice things like I remind him of the best parts of Franny Glass (knowing someone else might get all bent out of shape about this but that I appreciate the personally designed offbeat compliment) and he tells me he's so happy I agreed to be his girlfriend (he says *girlfriend* in my fantasies, repeatedly) and we talk about the future and I don't have that feeling of dread like I always do when they talk about the future. I know that when Donovan and I talk about the future in my fantasies there is an actual future, and he kisses me on the head and usually he makes breakfast and that I like my bacon well-done and remembers how I take my coffee.

Of course, you've probably already figured out that he had a girlfriend. Why Jason failed to mention this I've no idea. "I didn't think it mattered?"—Jason often said things like this with a grin, a low giggle, and a long drag on a cigarette. "No, I didn't know you liked him that much," he said.

"I think he's my soul mate."

"You don't believe in soul mates."

"*I know*," I said, "that's the thing."

Jason said he didn't think Donovan and Harumi were that serious (Why? Why? Why always Harumi or Sasha or Noelle or Birgitta or something? Why never Debbie or Becky? Or Shirley? My self-esteem could stand to make a huge gain in the face of a Shirley as my competition.) and that I should just ask him out. I reminded Jason I wasn't a boyfriend-stealer. "Hey," he said, "they're not married. It's all above-board at this point, I say."

I didn't ask him out. But after weeks of this non-flirting on the Diatribe circuit he ended up asking me if I wanted to go get some coffee after a show at the Empty Bottle. He told me up front that he was seeing someone but that he was really enjoying getting to know me and suggested maybe we could have a conversation that didn't involve second-hand smoke and ear-plugs. On the way out I whispered in Jason's ear, "I can't believe you told him," and he said, "Something had to be said."

Donovan and I went to the Hollywood Diner (way too bright at two in the morning for anyone's good, but open) and talked more about books we love and how he started drumming on pretty much any available surface when he was a kid (he openly admits to being heavily into Duran Duran when he was about eleven—do they even have a drummer?) and we really did talk about chemistry (you don't realize it, but it has everything to do with everything, apparently) and he told me a little about Harumi (not so much that any of my insecurities went into overdrive), mostly to insist that he and Harumi weren't exclusive, and to point out what he feels like he already has with me that he doesn't have with Harumi—I finally told him I didn't mind him talking about her but that he had to just stop saying her name; I explained why and he smiled like somehow this was endearing to him. He said we had some kind of deep connection. (He tried to explain it with a chemical analogy, which I only sort of got, but he was rather passionate about it as a concept, which just made me like him more.) I'd have gone home with him long before the whole subject of our scientific love came up (okay, my term, not his) about two hours later when he invited me over; there was some discussion about what a bad idea it might be, what with Harumi and all, but I'm pretty sure we both knew how it was going to end up when we left the Bottle. He said he just wanted to sleep next to me, which of course I've heard before, but as I was walking out of the diner he put his arms around me and put his head into the back of my neck and in that moment I knew he *would* just sleep next to me (assuming I had any ability to control myself on occasions when this line is spoken, which I usually don't).

Okay, and I don't know if his expertise in science had anything to do with it, but I think maybe he did have a more advanced notion than most about physical responses to stimuli,

because he paid particular attention to areas occasionally ne-
glected by the less scientific types I've known. I might go so far
as to say he made possible interactions I didn't know were possible. It was quite a bit better than I had fantasized about. When
Donovan left for work in the morning he told me to sleep in,
borrow any clothes I wanted to, and he gave me a key to lock up.
I held the gleaming key in my fingers and had a whole new series
of *Hi-honey-I'm-home*, key-based fantasies. He said he'd call me
later on my cell and he did.

I happened to be in his closet when he called. I ended up
sleeping until about two and was just getting around to looking
for something to wear when he rang. He said he had a great time
talking to me last night. *Talking* to me! He had that quiet voice.
He asked if he could see me again. I said that he could. He asked
if he could do those things to me again in the future. I said that
he could. He ended up telling me at some length exactly what
things he was talking about and embellished some more on top
of that and I can't say I'm really a big fan of phone sex but something about that closet, it was almost like he was there, maybe
better. I pulled a white oxford shirt off a hanger. It smelled like
lemons. The whole closet smelled like lemons. It wasn't really
even all that neat, there was a pile of laundry on the floor, and
nothing seemed to be folded or hung with any care. Which kind
of went along with his style—he had a sort of rumply thing going on. I looked for some evidence of lemons or lemon-scented
something. I thought maybe it was something of Harumi's, and
the smell was so amazing I might not even have minded if it
did trace back to some other girl, but I didn't come across any-

thing girly. There were boxes of antique chemistry sets. Most of them no longer had their original contents but instead were filled with memorabilia, a little plastic helicopter, photos, old cufflinks, miscellaneous postcards, and bundles of letters from his dad dating back about twenty years. I resisted what was only a small urge to snoop further. It wasn't the main attraction to me. It wasn't even the lemon scent, although that was somewhat intoxicating. It was like I found something I didn't even know I was looking for.

As soon as Donovan hung up, I called Jason to give him a report. "Where are you? The signal isn't too good."

"I'm in his closet."

"In whose closet?"

"Donovan's."

"What are you doing in his closet?"

"Do you want to hear about this or not?"

"Why don't you call me when you get home?"

"I don't know, I might hang here for a little while."

"In Donovan's closet."

"Yeah, it's just really nice."

"So?" (Phone drag/giggle combo, grin implied.)

"It was good. There will be more. There already has been more."

"Nice."

I fell asleep on the laundry. Fortunately, Donovan had band practice after work. It was the best sleep I've ever had. I dreamt of lemons and babies that looked like the best parts of Donovan and me, sleeping on shearling blankets. I put on the shirt and brought myself to leave and then I did something I didn't expect to do.

I copied the key.

Not only did I copy the key, I told the key copier that I was moving in with my new boyfriend. I told him I was pregnant and that we didn't believe in marriage in the conventional sense but that we were planning a Hindu ceremony at the Oak Street beach and that we were going to have twins and name them Akbar and Coyote if they were boys and Esme and Olive if they were girls. I told him Akbar was my deceased father's name and that I was an architect and that we were going to move as soon as the mountaintop hideaway was finished. I may have gone too far, or maybe it didn't matter, I don't think he could hear me over the key cutter anyway.

Donovan and I started spending more and more time together. It was not at all unlike my earlier fantasies. We did the crossword, listened to NPR, and he did explain stuff to me just like I said, kindly. He wore cotton pj's, just the bottoms mostly (he was tall and skinny but he was a tiny bit soft around the middle, which just killed me in the best way), and he remembered stuff, and he said crazy nice things like he told me I reminded him of this favorite story of his called "Little Red," which he tried to explain as being some kind of weird spin on *Little Red Riding Hood*, but the thing of it was mainly that the greatness of the story made him feel like there was a rightness in the world. "Like you do," he said.

People don't say stuff like that to me. At this juncture in the relationship is usually when people start pulling away so I'll break up with them. I've never really gone past this juncture before. The only time I ever reached this juncture at all, the guy broke up with me about three days after he told me he thought he was falling in love with me. When he suddenly stopped calling and I asked him what was going on, why he'd backed off just after he'd said that, he answered, "Yeah, I think I probably shouldn't have said that."

I started spending more time in his closet. My office was fairly close to Donovan's, so sometimes on my lunch break I went over for a nap. Sometimes I brought a book. It was a great place to read. There was a light, and it wasn't quite as big as a walk-in, but it was enviably roomy. Though it wasn't any of that, really, it was just the magic of the closet, like I said. Sometimes if Donovan seemed like he wanted to have phone sex I'd tell him I'd call him back and run over so I could be in the closet. It was just better in there. I tried not to take advantage by staying for more than an hour or two at a time. I didn't think I was hurting anyone. I didn't take anything and I didn't snoop. Once he came home on his lunch break—that was bad—and he made a phone call in the other room and I thought maybe he was talking to Harumi but it could have been my imagination, and I tried not to listen. I mean, I wanted to, but I didn't want to have any resentments, based on what? I was in his closet. Plus, he'd already told me he ended it with her about a day after our first sleepover. I closed the door and caught sight of my reflection in the mirror. It was the first time I'd ever bothered to close the door. It was not a good mirror. It was the closet's only flaw. It looked like I hadn't slept for a week and my skin seemed yellow. And not jaundice yellow. Lemon yellow.

I never mentioned the closet to Donovan. This went on for a while. Then I found myself sort of unsatisfied outside of the closet, even when I was with Donovan, even though everything was inconceivably good with Donovan, sometimes even if I was with Donovan in Donovan's bed, three feet from the closet. I started breaking plans with friends to be in the closet. I took longer and longer lunch breaks and used up all my sick days in the space of three weeks. I started forgetting things. Once, I woke up in the closet with no memory of having gone in there in the first place. I tried just carrying around one of his shirts or something else from the closet, but it was a poor substitute, and I tried my own closet but I couldn't duplicate the lemon scent or the feeling I had at Donovan's. Still, I thought I could leave the closet anytime. It wasn't like things weren't going well in the relationship. In fact, ever since the story thing I was fairly sure he was falling in love with me even though he hadn't said it, and it wasn't like I'd ever seen it before to know what it looked like. I was sure I was falling in love with him, at the very least, and that he seemed not to mind (a major improvement given my history of dating people who minded everything). At first I thought Donovan had no idea—he never said anything. He didn't seem to be pulling away on the schedule I was used to and he was so attentive, asking me if everything was okay, and were we okay, like he was afraid *I'd* end the relationship. And I came so close to telling him, because he really seemed like he'd understand. Once I opened the closet and he'd left me a copy of *A Prayer For Owen Meany* on a tray with a plate of cookies and a flower. I felt like Nicolas Cage in *Leaving Las Vegas*, when Elisabeth Shue gives him the flask. He'd officially given me a key a few weeks after he'd given it to me the first time, so it wasn't even like I was sneaking in anymore. But I couldn't stop.

I was addicted to Donovan's closet. It was like any other addiction but there was no program for me. Jason eventually figured it out. He said, "Have you been hanging out in Donovan's closet?" It was admittedly a weird accusation when spoken out loud.

"What do you mean?"

"You smell like lemons and laundry and you missed our last two shows."

I made some excuses but I kind of messed up when I told him I wasn't doing it that much and that I could handle it.

Jason took a long pause and finally said, "Let's go shopping."

I told him I didn't feel like shopping.

That was probably a mistake. He knew it was a bleak day if I wasn't in the mood to shop. Then he said, "I'll be over in ten minutes." I didn't have to mention I was at Donovan's. He found me in the closet in a pair of Donovan's sweatpants and my hair in a scrunchie. He gently pulled the scrunchie out and smoothed out my hair. "I had no idea it had gotten this bad." He handed me a brush and we drove straight over to Barney's.

In the men's department, Jason called over a shoe sales-man (they knew each other by name) and asked him to tell Mel he was here. Mel, a middle-aged man in a navy Jil Sander suit, came out from the back room and hugged Jason like they were old friends. Jason introduced me to Mel, who shook my hand

and smiled warmly. "Mel's my personal shopper," he explained.

"Welcome," Mel said, which I thought was a funny thing to be saying at Barney's, the way he said it, anyway. It was like he was welcoming me to some kind of fraternity. Plus, we were still in the men's department, which I didn't have much use for. "Come on back," he said, leading us across the store. He leaned into Jason's ear. "I have some nice things for you when she gets settled." Jason nodded. "I'll let you show her in from here." Jason led me into a secluded dressing area reserved for special customers. It was exquisite. Like a spa. It didn't smell like lemons, but I will say I had a little bit of that closet feeling almost as soon as I walked in. It was all white with a skylight even and there was a huge over-stuffed chair with an ottoman in one corner I settled myself right into. The shoe salesman came in with a glass of wine and a small cheese platter and then he and Jason left me alone. I thought maybe someone would bring me some clothes at some point, but no one ever came and I was kind of hoping they wouldn't anyway. They just let me stay until I was ready to come out. I had a little wine and cheese and fell asleep in the chair.

When I got up I felt like I'd had a week's vacation. I caught my reflection in the giant three-way mirror (always a potential danger even knowing they're usually skinny mirrors) and it looked like me, but if I were a movie star, I was almost sparkly. I'm not sure how long I was in there and for sure I can't tell you what exactly happened, but I just felt better.

Afterward I had a long talk with Mel. I confessed about Donovan's closet like Mel was a priest, and he was cool. Mostly he just listened. I had the impression he'd heard weirder things.

He told me to feel free to come back anytime. It was an amazing place, and I told him I'd like to, but I had a feeling I wouldn't need to. It was like something got lifted. Then we shopped. It was an all-around good day.

After that I was still drawn to the closet, I won't tell you I wasn't, but I didn't need it so much anymore. I never told Donovan about the closet but I did tell him that I was pretty sure I had a spiritual experience in the dressing room at Barney's. And I tell you, he did not even laugh. He could have, I was even sort of giggling when I said it. We didn't talk much about that kind of stuff. (Spiritual experiences or even Barney's, for that matter.) I figured it wasn't his thing, being scientific and all, that maybe he'd judge me, but he didn't. He kissed me on the head.

Right after that I consulted the *Magic 8 Ball* key ring again about our future. My eye landed on *No*, but it was on the line again between that and *Yes*, and when I looked closer, the *No* I'd seen was followed by the word *Doubt*. It was on the line between *Yes* and *No Doubt*.

SALLY

(FEATURING: LOLLIPOP THE RAINBOW UNICORN)

THERE IS NOT ONE THING even a little bit sad about this story. This is pretty much the happiest story ever. If you're all up into *War and Peace* or whichever, you won't find it here.

This story is about a woman who was always herself. What better story could there be than that? Plus it's true, or mostly true. It's true enough. It's true-seeming.

One presumes that Sally, is her name, started out being a girl who was always herself. You have heard it told that she was herself as a teenager, so it's a logical conclusion, even if it is hard to imagine. Because do you know any teenagers who are themselves? I doubt it. Teenagers are all about being other people. You so wish you'd known her when you were a teenager, but she was born in the '70s, so she would have been in preschool at the time. Although Sally at four was probably more you than you are after all the therapy. You don't really know much about her life as a preschooler, so you don't know whether her parents did anything really right or really wrong, and my feeling is that it doesn't really matter. My feeling is that Sally became Sally regardless of whether or not her parents did anything right or wrong. And I'm not talking about genetics either, since I don't know thing one about that. Let's just put it like this: On the day Sally was born, the stars collided or the planets aligned or the people stepped over the cracks and it worked out how it did. All you know is, maybe if you had even babysat for her or something, your life could have gone a different way. You could possibly have learned from her even then with regard to being yourself. I realize you're fine now, but there were some ineffective years. We both know it.

So but look at Sally. She's *That Girl* looking at herself in the store window and seeing versions of herself all around the city, except if *That Girl* had an eyebrow ring, big boots, and was a happy, funny revolutionary and there were no Donald Hollingers. Nothing that looks like Donald Hollinger, nothing that acts like Donald Hollinger, no ex–Donald Hollinger to be gotten rid of. No Donald Hollinger of any kind. It's not that she doesn't enjoy the company of men, you have heard that she does, it's not even that she wouldn't like the company of a nice man, you have heard this as well, it's simply that having a man, even a nice one, is not critical to her being completely, joyfully Sally. This, to you, is only theoretical. To you it's something to hope for, but you are not feeling so completely joyfully you without a Mr. You. Seventy-eight percent joyful on a good day, maybe, which is an improvement over other times in your life, but still. Do you see what I'm saying? Do you know anyone like this? Probably not. But you should know Sally. You should *be* Sally. Fine, be yourself. But like Sally.

From what you know, Sally as a teenager had, like, beliefs. She had things that she *believed in*. I know, what's that all about, right? But she did, and Sally made a decision not to ever compromise her beliefs, which is, well, come on, who's ever done that? Not me and not you, because it's hard, think about it, think about all the seemingly small compromises you've made in the category of people you've dated alone. It's hard to know which choice was worse, Gene the judgmental environmentalist (judgmenvironmentalist?) or Philip who thought it was his right to park illegally without paying tickets because *his taxes more than covered it*, which on his salary from Quiznos you can be sure they did not. And how about that time you didn't tell them they forgot to scan your Lucky Charms at the grocery store and you told yourself the fact that they happened to be called "Lucky Charms" was a sign that it was okay, just this one time. Or that time you ate a Quarter Pounder (with cheese!) after you swore you'd never eat at McDonald's again after reading *Fast Food Nation*. Or spending actual cash money on a copy of *Star* magazine on impulse at the supermarket checkout because on the cover it alleged a prurient relationship between Jake and Maggie Gyllenhaal even though inside the title read, *Jake and Maggie: Siblings!* which is what they always do and you should have known it, and you felt positively greasy afterward even though it was only ninety-nine cents, because you have to live with knowing that ninety-nine cents of your money went to perpetuating more of the same. (Not to mention more fanciful scenarios like let's say if some huge low-priced chain store that was known to use child labor in sweatshops offered you three million dollars to be in their new ad campaign, at the very least you wouldn't just say no flat out and probably you would even think, *Hell yes, what values?* first before you thought the whole thing through to the point where you were possibly conflicted but were leaning toward a complex, supposedly ethical justification for going through with it.) What about being best friends with Jessica Sandler in third grade because her dad took you to FAO Schwartz and bought you a Little Kiddle even though Jessica Sandler was kind of spoiled and bratty, and even though she was mostly nice to you she was often mean to other people. Who wouldn't be friends with Jessica Sandler for a Little Kiddle? Sally. Is who. No way would Sally sell out for a Little Kiddle. Sally was disappointed in the world, a bit, but not in a dark despairing, *Oh, I'll just go mope around to a Morrissey record* teenager kind of way, in a *You know, I might be able to do a little something about this* kind of way.

Which is what she did. And you can imagine why, because who wouldn't listen to such an engaging, funny chick? We already know how easily influenced you are, what with your Jessica Little Kiddle history, so imagine what might happen if you met up with Sally, and she charmed you like she charmed me, and she said, *There's this thing wrong with the world and this is what I tried to do about it*, and whatever her story happens to be that day, because she has a lot of them, it will in some way be funny, and this story will make you feel like changing the world actually is possible, in bits and pieces anyway. What you especially admire about her is the way she's not all righteous or whichever, she's not even, *You kinda need to go do some stuff too*. But it will happen because she's that compelling. You will want to do what you can do. Try not to be disappointed if it doesn't seem as cool as what Sally's doing. Not possible. Making art is not unimportant. Tell yourself that. No seriously, try.

Sally got her hand in like sixteen pies from the get go. Seventeen if you count actual pies, which is something Sally enjoys and partakes in frequently. Zines and what have you. *Princess Vanessa Lipstick McGillicuddy Tells the Truth*, her first zine, is legendary in certain circles. In zine-reading circles. You didn't even know what a zine was before Sally. Sally is the kind of person who let's just say for example if there's an awful war going on, or if large numbers of people and even corporations are opposed to similarly gendered people getting married, or if people are opposed to other people having opinions that are different than those people's opinions, or if people are listening in on your phone calls and reading your e-mails and calling it security, or I don't know what else, unlike me and you, she won't be like, *What am I gonna do, go march or something? Because crowds freak me out and plus what's the point?* Sally might march or she might not, but what she will do is hang around the White House holding a bunch of balloons, smiling, and get reporters to ask her why she is hanging around the White House holding a bunch of balloons, and then cheerfully tell them it seemed like a pleasant way to say she was against the war and would they like a balloon? Or maybe she'd do something like go into elementary schools calling herself "Storyteller Princess Vanessa Lipstick

McGillicuddy" and then read fairy tales and other books that she'd rewritten to get little girls to rethink the whole happy ending needing to have a dude in it or that a Barbie-shaped body would be a sort of effective emotional problem-solver of any kind and that maybe a happy ending was one where you stood outside the White House with a bunch of balloons. And more pies like this. Pies that never even occurred to you.

A little-known fact about Sally is that she has several situation-specific superpowers. Let's go back to the White House, for example. Sally might discover, upon leaning against the front gates, that she suddenly had a rubbery quality that would allow her to slip right through. Think of the possibilities! I mean, rubbery is not the same as invisible, but if she could get through, think of what she could do on the inside of the White House with all those balloons! They wouldn't know what to do. They would be all, *This lady with a pierced eyebrow came into the White House and gave out balloons!* And someone with a lick of sense, like maybe a guard or a secretary who has no interest in party lines or anything, just wants to make her Kia payments, says, *So?* And everyone else would go, *So? So? So?* And the lick-of-sense lady would say, *Yes, so?* as in "so what?" and the White House people would be like, *You can't just give out balloons around here*, but no one can say why, exactly, or find a law that says you can't, which is what they run around trying to do while Sally waits patiently in the office of the press secretary, who listens to her opinion about the war and being against it, and exactly why, and this gets relayed to the media via the press secretary because that's their job, press secretaries, to explain things to the press like how people with balloons get into the White House but to try to tell it in a way that it seems threatening but that they have it under control and even though they believe in freedom of speech they don't believe in, well, balloons, maybe. You don't know.

On the rubbery front, she discovered while rehearsing for a school reading that she could grow herself a Barbie body. Freakish to be sure, but what a perfect illustration of how wrong that is, to see a Barbie body on a real person! Besides not wanting to freak the kids out, Sally feels like even she isn't immune to abusing her superpowers. Like if there were some two thousand–dollar pair of the cutest big boots ever and she had the ability to psychically make salespeople offer her a ninety percent discount, she knows she might do it. Plus, even Sally doesn't really know what all her superpowers are. Sometimes they just show up. Like the rubbery. The thing that's important about this fact is that she doesn't use them. She doesn't think it's fair. *I'd use them if I were really in trouble,* she says. *But I haven't had to yet.*

Fine. Maybe this is less true than I led you to believe at the outset. Maybe she doesn't have superpowers. Maybe she kicked a boy in the knee once in grade school. Maybe he deserved it. Maybe she's lonely, maybe her mom makes her completely nuts sometimes. Maybe her dad reads the paper during dinner. Maybe she doubts herself on occasion. Doesn't matter. All the better if one or more are true, then there's more hope for you. You don't think so. But you don't need to know.

Anyway, then you find her. No, she finds you. She thinks

there's something about *you*. How is *that* possible? *Because of the art*, she tells you, even though you hadn't said that out loud. To which you say, *But that's what I like to do*. To which she says, *No kidding*. To which you say, *Well then*, and, *hm*.

Finally one day she tells you a story about how she goes to the park with her new kite, and her new kite has a rainbow unicorn on it she named Lollipop, except it's not very windy on this day so Lollipop isn't getting a lot of air, except Sally doesn't really mind, because she is cracking herself up that she has a kite with a rainbow unicorn named Lollipop. It's like the most perfect image of actual joy you've ever heard of, forget babies in pumpkins or whatever, this is a grown woman frolicking and cracking herself up with a kite and a unicorn. It should be on the cover of a magazine, except it isn't, because the magazines are clogged up with Angelina Jolie always, as though there's no one else, and maybe Angelina Jolie isn't a role model for every girl or woman, do you see? Maybe the world would like other options. And you can relate, because sometimes you crack yourself up, which is probably why you like her.

WHAT HAPPENS WHEN THE MIPODS
LEAVE THEIR MILIEU

THIS IS THE SORT OF THING Shane Mipod hears at the department luncheon: "Shane Mipod—Thomas Wheathrop, Associate Ble Mmmh Fffh in Baaa Rum Glurr." Shane, a recent winner of the Jeep Prize for his graphic novel, *Amen*, has just been hired as an adjunct lecturer at Prestimia College. Shane's entire resume exists in the previous sentence, unless you include sixteen odd jobs and twenty-four credits from Laszlow Community College and some freelance work in graphic design. He's a bright enough guy, but to say this is not his milicu would be an understatement. To say that he has no milieu at all would be more like it. How he got this job is the dean's assistant raved about the book and the dean saw *Jeep Prize* on the back and called Shane up totally out of the blue and offered him a job. "Send us your CV right away," the dean had said. "Just as a formality, of course," and Shane, needing a job and never in his wildest dreams imagining that the dean of anything would hire him for anything, thanked him, hung up the phone, and yelled into the other room, "Honey? What's a CV?"

"Isn't that like a mobile home or something?" said his wife, Honey.

"I think that's an RV."

Here is a brief sampling of what could be on the aforementioned CV, if resumes by Latin names included such things: waiter, assistant at a law firm (Shane types 65 wpm and is additionally skilled at the Dictaphone), assistant at an auto parts factory, assistant at a conglomerate he was unclear about the nature of, comic book salesman, assistant at a startup felt-tip pen company, dog walker, nanny, and, now, college professor. (Briefly, Honey will refer to him as her "own private nanny and the professor.")

Each of these milieus, if you will, has a considerably different bunch of people present. In each of these places Shane has wondered what he was doing there and in each of these places Shane has had moments of feeling like he totally belonged, but some of the places where you might think he belonged— basically anyplace where people look the most like him, which is to say not very extremely anything—places such as let's just say Prestimia, where with certain exceptions one sees a lot of people in neutral tones, which are tones Shane is heavily invested in so as to better achieve a blending-in, a sort of you-can't-go-too-wrong-with-neutral-tones-anywhere line of thinking, and yet these are precisely the sorts of places where Shane ends up feeling the lowest sense of belonging. This lack of belonging anywhere in the world may explain Shane's need for a spiritual fellowship, and it may also explain why the Mipods have tended to live in largely Hispanic neighborhoods. Shane suspects that the people in his neighborhood don't think much about him at all, which only serves to emphasize his conundrum.

At the luncheon Shane is mostly quiet. He shakes a lot of hands and smiles and nods and thanks the two people at the long table that had read and enjoyed his book, but struggles to silence a third *awesome* from his mouth before it escapes. He may not be in his milieu, but is aware that these are not people inclined toward this casual type of enthusiasm. Randomly he hears other words, like *pedagogy* and *canonical* and *colloquium* and *tempered*, but is unable to contribute much to the conversation in the way of fresh content. Occasionally he will hear a word, one like *syllabus* or even *expedient*, that he can process into something tangible, but this is sporadic at best. Fortunately, one of the other adjuncts, a sculptor who works in air, knows this sort of virgin when she sees one, and invites him outside for a cigarette. Shane starts to explain to her that he doesn't smoke, but she quietly stares him down into complying. "Neither do I," she whispers.

Outside, not smoking, she says, "Here's what you need to know."

Shane's thinking it would help to know her name, but is afraid to ask.

"The tall guy with the weird skin thing is the current Blog Laureate. He does not meet eyes with people. It's not because he's tall. The largeish woman with the turquoise pashmina is head of Cross-Departmental Genre. She's never not in a mood.

The dude with the wool socks and sandals, I swear he's just here to fill that stereotype, I don't know what he does, but I know he's sleeping with Bridget from the registrar's office, and that he's married and thinks no one knows but actually everyone knows. Which is something else you should know. Everyone knows everything, except what any of us actually do. You think that doesn't make sense, which it doesn't, nevertheless it's true."

He knows he should say something soon, but doesn't know what.

"Oh, and I'm the big old lesbian. Do you want to have coffee next week? I can fill you in more then."

"There's more?"

"Um, yeah. There's more."

Shane agrees to the coffee but musters the courage to insist she reveal her name.

"Marjorie Vision-Specter, sorry."

"Marjorie—do we like anyone here?" is what Shane finally says.

Marjorie chuckles. "Actually, we do. We like quite a few people."

Shane is relieved, for the time being.

He returns home to Honey, who he met when he was floundering at LCC. Shane and Honey Mipod are devout believers. Honey runs the office at Church and *Amen* is more or less a chronicle of their early romance.

What they believe is kind of hard to explain, sort of a smorgasbord of beliefs, a big serving of Zen, a heap each of Judaism, Christianity, and Hinduism, mythology, a lot of love thy neighbor, no Kabbalah whatsoever, not even a little Scientology, not so much of the hell that exists in an actual and hot location, efforts at patience and tolerance and understanding and charity and forgiveness, a measure of doubt for good measure. Their motto, *We don't pretend to know everything,* is carved into a wood-grain panel on the front door. They are ardently against putting alcoholic beverages of any kind into the body, as they believe in living consciously, although they tend to favor rituals for virtually any life change, big or small, one of which involves sacramental pot-smoking. For another example, purchases over fifty dollars call for a ceremonial bell-ringing, which does not go unnoticed at Wal-Mart, and is the sort of thing that calls their overall legitimacy into question for a lot of folks. What they believe doesn't involve a person with a gender or a face, but it doesn't not, either. They call their god G for one reason: it's short. There was a period, at the dawning of the politically correct era, when members were encouraged to use variants of the pronoun "he or she" as necessary, but this proved clunky and sometimes confusing, and failed to address the gender/non-gender issue anyway. Their church is just called Church. It has been derided as being too much of too many things, too little of anything definite, and way too new to count.

They don't practice this perfectly, ever, but they always believe. If Shane does have a milieu, Church would be it, although he might like to think the world is everyone's milieu.

Oh, also, they lean mostly to the left, politically. The Mipods. Church-Goers, as they're known, are free to associate themselves with any political party, and do not tend to lean one way or another as a group, although it is widely believed that they generally lean to the right, which is erroneous. They lean however they lean, which is many ways. Anyway, Shane's book, remember it's called *Amen*, has some strong religious themes, and follows Shane's life from before he met Honey, when he was kind of a partier, albeit a quiet one who tended to go to a dorm party for an hour just to get a buzz and then go back to his room and doodle talking skulls, to meeting Honey in the quad on the campus of Laszlow on a sleeting winter day when she was trying to witness for the Church but no one was spending more seconds outside than they had to. Feeling her pain as much as a stoned guy is able to, Shane went and talked to her, and her being very obviously cute made his lack of gloves slightly more bearable, and so he agreed to go to Church that Sunday even though he was at the time, remember, kind of into skulls and beer. He was, however, a virgin, which is something the Church recommends, and although it was hardly by choice, he ended up deciding to hold onto it after Church that first time, because it made sense to him that making love was not to be entered into casually, that there had to be more to it than what it sounded like coming from the closet in his dorm room, which was where his roommate Kip brought girls. Plus, truth be told, although he was horny, the idea of doing it only became more frightening to him as time passed. In the end, he didn't hold onto it all that long, because within a year he and Honey fell in love, married, and had clumsy sex that was occasionally mind-blowing enough for both of them to want to keep doing it. But the Church still made sense to him in a logical kind of way, so he became a deacon, dropped out of school, and felt more hopeful about life than he could have imagined was possible without beer. What he had not expected was the backlash.

Out in the world, he and Honey find themselves at odds with people, find witnessing, which they were once so eager to do, painful, find themselves increasingly hesitant to mention that they love G the way they do, find that people are usually stunned to hear that the Mipods actually accept gays, that they are in favor of stem cell research, that they are against the war, that they are not fond of the president, that Shane once voted straight down the Green ticket. They aren't so sure about abortion or the death penalty, they kind of think that life and death things aren't really up to them, but Shane and Honey both have to admit that if anyone were to harm their child, born or unborn, they might at least picture that person bleeding to death slowly and alone.

When the term begins, it takes a few classes before Shane hits his stride. Because of his awareness that many of his students are already more educated than he is, Shane cannot help but feel concerned about what he has to offer. He has, of course, never taught before, but he does know how to draw and how to write, and as it turns out, has an unassuming but natural way of talking about process without actually using the word *process*, which is one more word Shane knows primarily from another context: he knows what it means when placed in front of a word like *cheese*. In Shane's class, process is called "This is how I do it, although you might do it another way, and that's fine." The class, which had filled up as soon as it was announced, is the talk of a certain brainy-geeky portion of the student body known to spend considerable time online and/or in comic-book stores. Unbeknownst to Shane, they feel as though they are enrolled in the comics equivalent of class with a rock star, and it isn't that Shane is unaware that his work has been well-received, but he doesn't read reviews, spends little time online himself, drawing in any spare moment, and hasn't done more than a handful of readings, which were all before *Amen* had come out. Also, he's just kind of not terribly tuned in to how people see him. Shane's feeling tends to be that people generally don't see him at all, which perhaps had some accuracy before *Amen*, but which has changed and which Shane is more or less oblivious to. In some ways, Shane sort of wishes he were *in* the class instead of teaching it. He hadn't gotten a lot in the way of art at Laszlow Community College.

Nevertheless he is teaching it, and after the first few classes in which students are feeling a bit shy, he finally backtracks and gets everyone to start talking about who their favorite comics artists are, which breaks the ice because there are a few very different opinions about this and gets everyone all worked up and able to see that Shane is just another person who read *Fantastic Four* and *The Tick* when he was a kid and is someone who they don't have to agree with or even like in order to learn from, although they do, both, like him and learn from him. Over the term, his students' work shows significant improvement, and Shane has the briefest moments of feeling that he may be in his milieu, or at least a milieu where he's welcome to stop by.

One of his students is this kid Marque (pronounced

Mark)—to describe him as awkward would not quite capture the precise components of his awkwardness, nor his particular charm. Marque is not lacking for friends, and from a block away you might identify him as something of a hipster, with kind of overgrown Beatles hair and thrift-shop sweaters from the '80s and a certain kind of tilty posture, that sort of posture that announces to the world the painful fact that the person in the somewhat slouchy but sort of inflexible posture is in a certain metaphorical way not exactly occupying the space that is his body, the kind of person who has a singular way of thinking but is unable to make that singular mind work properly within a human vehicle with moving limbs and such. Nevertheless, anything hipsterish about Marque is entirely accidental. His sweaters are not actually from the thrift shop. They are new sweaters, hand knit by his mother, primarily involving wide stripes in combinations like bright orange and brown, with scratchy labels inside that say, *Made Just 4 U With* ♥.

Anyway, Marque feels that he needs extra help and arranges to meet Shane at the campus coffee shop. As it turns out, the kind of help Marque needs is not so much related to his progress in the class but is more personal in nature. Marque has of late been coming to recognize the disparity between his body and his mind, and admires the sense of serenity he observes in Shane, although Shane isn't sure he'd agree unless by comparison to Marque, who kind of makes Shane look like some sort of Yoda. Shane, naturally, would love to invite Marque to Church, but having read some of Marque's wildly illustrated class work at this point, knows that Marque's idea of god is that god is a bit of a jerk, which is an idea founded on his mom's perpetual spiritual post-game analysis, if you will, of just about any event in their lives big or small, surmising that no event is untouched by the hand of the lord, really, not your more obvious miracles like healthy babies and not even your lesser miracles such as your dad staying sober for a whole twenty-four hours and not whacking your mom into the neighbor's yard, which Marque sees not so much as a blessed day but suspects that to most people is just *a day*. Not only that, but Shane has some serious reservations about whether or not inviting a student to Church is appropriate. Shane suggests maybe cutting back on caffeine, based on having noticed that Marque tends to have with him at all times a gallon-sized mug full of Coke, the kind truck drivers use, but really, he doesn't suppose that will make a huge difference, or that Marque is prepared to make the shift anyway. The meeting is not especially productive.

So here's Shane and Honey at the semi-annual Humanities cocktail party. Of course, there is no graphic novel department at Prestimia, which is why he's been lumped into Cross-Departmental, which is where they lump everyone who doesn't fit very neatly into any one department. Which right now consists of him, Marjorie Vision-Specter, and a floet. Malena Greer, the woman in the turquoise pashmina, is presently raving about Shane's work, and although it's clear that she doesn't really get it, she is in the middle of explaining it to several colleagues. "The man simply blows irony out of the water," she says. At this point Shane is not catching Malena's meaning. In fact, his work rejects irony altogether, although he probably doesn't know it. Irony is virtually nonexistent in his world. He recognizes that Malena in the pashmina means to pay him a compliment, but it is one he isn't getting. "It's meta-irony. It's an audacious parody of the Church, satire on a whole new level." The colleagues chuckle knowingly. They say things like, *"God," "Ha ha," "Yes, yes,"* and *"Brilliant,"* all in italics. The italics are practically visible above their heads, inside little thought balloons. Not that anyone here talks any other way. Marjorie Vision-Specter and Shane Mipod being the unsurprising exceptions. Marjorie considers explaining, because she gets it, but instead just rolls her eyes to herself. She has never liked Malena, though she does like her job.

Honey is somewhat intimidated by Malena for any number of reasons, including her pashmina, but makes an attempt to pipe in. "Um, well," is about all she has a chance to say before a man dressed in a clown costume carrying a bunch of balloons, obviously lost, peeks in the doorway.

"Perfect!" says Malena. "That is *the* perfect representation of what I'm talking about." She pronounces "the" as "theee"— with at least three Es, maybe four. In fact, no one in the group really knows what she's talking about now, but what Shane doesn't know is that they are very good at acting like they do.

Honey has no idea what the clown could possibly be representing perfectly in this discussion, but tries to finish her original thought. "I'm not sure . . . It's just that . . . Will you excuse us for a moment?" Honey pulls Shane over to the punch bowl. "Baby, it might not be my place to testify here, but I don't think these people are feeling you, and I don't much care for hearing the story of our love referred to as a parody." Shane concurs that they seem not to get it, but reminds Honey that he's new and doesn't want to jeopardize his position, seeing as how they're trying to save for their future baby's college fund. A little known fact is that the prestigious Jeep Prize is simply a Jeep and a thousand-dollar *honorarium*. Which someone had to explain to Shane was, for his purposes, the same as "money."

"I'm just thinking about little Shanoney," he says, and Honey backs off, but with an "Alright" that doesn't sound like it's really alright.

When they return to the conversation, Malena is still dominating, finishing a sentence with "and that is everything that is wrong with religion in America today."

Shane quietly asks about the part of the sentence he missed. Malena in the pashmina says, "Everything your work disavows about religion, the exclusivity, the bizarro rituals, the sexual dark ages, the right-wing plotting . . ."

Honey blurts out, "*Amen* isn't a disavowal."

Malena actually takes a breath before she speaks, simply because this seems unthinkable. Finally, "Surely you're joking."

"No," Shane says. He goes on to politely explain that his work is not ironic, that it was his attempt to carry the message of love and hope that he has received so plentifully through the Church, and that he is currently feeling grave concern that he has failed.

Malena still does not understand. She thinks he is being ironic saying he is not ironic. She laughs loudly, tossing her pashmina back over her shoulder. "HAH!" It is only when none of the colleagues, now visibly uncomfortable, take her lead that she begins to realize the true lack of irony in Shane's irony.

Marjorie tries her best to explain to Malena the meaning of the word *sincere* without being sarcastic, but Malena, a linguistics professor, doesn't much appreciate it. "Yes, I know what sincerity is, thanks—you." Malena is hoping that the "s" on the end of her "thanks" and the brief pause after it that indicates that she does not know Marjorie's name, go unheard.

At this point, Malena is rendered temporarily silent, and when she finally excuses herself, the colleagues scatter.

Shane gets fired the following Monday, in the form of a terse e-mail.

From: malena.greer@prestimia.edu

To: Shanoney@yahoo.com

Re: Faculty

Things have come to our attention that call into question the relevance of your position here at Prestimia, and as such we regretfully and respectfully request that you remove your personal belongings from your office at once and return your key.

Shane doesn't have an office, or a key.

"Hey, Honey?"

"Yeah?"

"I think I just got fired, can you come look at this?"

"Hm. Yeah, I'm pretty sure you are fired. I think this is one of those letters that tries to say something by saying nothing."

"What 'things'? What are things?"

"I'm not sure, but apparently you have been fired for them."

"Can they do this?"

"I don't know."

"Am I irrelevant?"

"I don't think of you that way. I find you relevant."

"I'm in the middle of the term. What about my students? Do you think this has something to do with the party last week?"

Honey plays back the awkward conversation in her head. "Oh no, this is my fault."

"What?"

"I made you tell them you weren't ironic."

"Don't be ridiculous."

"No, think about it."

"You can't fire someone for their religious beliefs."

"Hence the mysterious 'things.'"

"Nuh uh!" says Shane, but they know it's really Yuh huh.

The Mipods don't know what to do now. They pray, but that's obvious. They perform the ceremonial job-firing dance, which involves burning the pink slip, or in this case, a printout of the terse e-mail, in a ceramic bowl labeled *Work*. (Kept on a shelf next to the other ceremonial bowls they burn things in and then dance around, including one labeled *Miscellaneous*.)

They go to Church. They bring their prayer request before the congregation, asking that they open up new opportunities to witness, that they open up new opportunities for work best suited to their desire to provide for the unconceived Shanoney in a way that compromises neither their spiritual beliefs nor their need for "a few nice things from JC Penney, nothing too much," and to bless everyone at Prestimia College, "especially Malena Greer, who seems like she needs it more than anyone."

Some time goes by. The Mipods are the kind of people who may be certain about how prayers are answered in their own lives, but posit theories about whether or not their prayers for others are also addressed by the big G. In this case, there seems to be little they can identify in the way of response from god. No work comes their way, although during this time, Shanoney is conceived in the form of twins, which they recognize as a blessing in spite of god not sending a Penney's gift card. So the Mipods posit theories all the way around this time. "Maybe G figures we don't need to be showed who to witness to," posits Shane. Upon glancing at a lottery winner on TV, "Maybe it's a numbers game," posits Honey. Upon no word about Malena Greer whatsoever, "Maybe G thinks we don't need to know," posits Shane. "Or maybe we're supposed to follow up?" Honey posits back.

Shortly after Shane's firing by terse e-mail, Marjorie mentions her outrage at the incident on her Livejournal, recounting, at some length, her memory of the cocktail party conversation that preceded and apparently hastened the demise of Shane's academic career, ranting about art and freedom of religion and freedom of speech and admittedly mixing in a few other issues of her own (why bad lesbian dates are worse than bad gay dates, details about what's wrong with her HMO, and how, "just for example," very few people appreciate art made of air) for good measure.

Marjorie, who writes all these things on her Livejournal because she believes it to be private, is wrong, because everyone knows you can Google a phrase and get sent to a private Live-journal, which is what happens when someone at one of the news blogs, looking for something else entirely, lands on Marjorie's Livejournal and immediately links to it, which is picked up by a news outlet, at which time it becomes one of those little stories that ends up being big news, kind of like when one person says *Elián González* and another says *Elián González* and then so many people say *Elián González* that even people who mostly avoid the news eventually hear someone say *Elián González*, maybe in con-versation, and so everyone around the world except for maybe Third World countries very quickly learn who Elián González is, which is all to say that Shane Mipod is, in this way and for a while, Elián González.

The Mipods are interviewed by many people, and to many people they testify. They say things like, "We hold no bitterness toward Prestimia College, even though we probably could, and maybe should, we don't, because part of our faith is to show compassion and understanding toward everyone at all times, and plus, we believe that some things happen for a reason, which in this case is pretty obviously so that we can share our hopeful message to many more people than we could just the usual way we do, which is just by walking around and talking to people one at a time or if they come by Church and talk to us or whatever." They learn the word *forum*, and it is suggested that they become televangelists, which they consider and reject on the basis of that never turning out to be very cool. Instead they start a blog of their own. BloG.

The next time they go to Church they thank the congregation for answering their prayers about witnessing.

Unfortunately, what ends up happening is that Shane and Honey and their fellows in the Church are misunderstood by people everywhere now.

One day Marque shows up at coffee after Church. Shane welcomes him with a hug. Marque does his best to lift his arms up and place them around Shane's back—it's a hug in name only, and for Marque it's not nothing.

"I've been following all the hooplah, and I realized how you got your mellow," Marque explains. Shane says he wishes now that he'd mentioned it to Marque that day at the café but that it didn't feel right.

This seems to Shane like one of those if-you-reach-one-person-you've-done-your-job kind of moments, even though really Marque is just as drawn in by the cute girl handing out the sticky buns, but which, if you think about it, is kind of how Shane came in. "Look, Honey," Shane says, pointing to Marque and the sticky bun girl, "I feel like it's coming full circle now." It's a happy day for the Mipods.

Except for them being broke and having no college fund for Shanoney.

EMMANUEL

FRANKLY, I DIDN'T THINK MY CHANCES WERE GOOD. I was over forty and it hadn't happened yet even though I'd been less-than-careful for pretty much ever. I suppose if you calculated a rough estimate of the actual number of times I've had sex over the years it might not be as substantial as one might think, given my age. Long-term relationships were never my specialty, plus before I met Sam I hadn't been with anyone in the biblical sense for several years. That was sort of a purposeful accident—after years of research I determined that I wasn't cut out for loveless sex, but had I known exactly how long I'd have to wait for love-filled sex I might not have held out as long as I did. Thankfully Sam came into the picture and was everything I hoped for. He was super cute and sweet and his steadfast belief in god, which is very important to me, was off the hook. While his was some-what of a different god than my own, like one with an identifi-able face, we came to believe that our different gods brought us together for spiritual learning and after about a year of dating he asked me to marry him and so we got married and started trying right away because of the whole clock thing and we prayed every day for my womb to be welcoming to any kind of a healthy baby and amazingly one of Sam's little swimmers found itself a home and we were so happy and grateful to god for our miracle baby. We decided to name it Loretta if it was a girl, after Loretta Lynn, and Emmanuel if it was a boy, which I learned from Sam reading the Bible to me means "God with us." I should say so.

Emmanuel was born healthy and fat and we sure did feel that god was with us and we thanked him every day. Emmanuel was as perfect as he could possibly be, with Sam's big blue eyes and my round butt which on a baby turns out to be very very cute and squeezable. Unlike me he had a small but unusual birthmark on his right butt cheek that looked almost uncannily like that symbol Prince used for his name before he went back to being Prince again. Emmanuel hardly ever cried and although I wouldn't say he smiled a lot he just had this happy look of wonder in his eyes that a baby has where everything in front of him is new and exciting, even if it's, like, Sam's super stank dirty work socks going into the washing machine or whatever. Sam's super stank anything was always a wonder to Emmanuel; as soon as he could crawl he lumbered right into the laundry pile and laughed and laughed. Anybody who thinks they have to get that stuff you see in, like, *Perfect Baby Monthly* or whatever, is both seriously misguided and wasting a whole bunch of money they could be giving to charity, because babies, I think I can say definitively, just do not know the difference between a stank sock and a Beanie

Baby. We got a whole bunch of hand-me-downs from friends and stuff from the thrift store because they grow and change with more or less the speed of light. Also we have a rule that if we ever spend four hundred dollars on something that isn't as big as, like, a car, like let's say a very darling baby lamp with tiny gold-leaf stars that I saw at Babies Babies Babies, then we have to also donate four hundred dollars to charity because it's only right. If however you follow the logic we are not generally in the position to be buying four-hundred-dollar lamps, and anyway Sam had the cutest little lamp from his childhood that he bought at an auction when he was seven or something that had a wooden statue of Charlie the Tuna holding up the lampshade, and guess what? It makes light just fine, and even though he didn't talk yet, Emmanuel never gave us any indication of disappointment in the lack of gold-leaf stars on his lamp.

I've gotten a little sidetracked here reminiscing about when Manny (that's what we called him) was a baby because it was such an enchanted time, but I should probably get to the point and tell you that one morning I went in to wake him up and our miracle baby wasn't a baby anymore. He was all grown up, scrunched into his crib, and he was asking to be called Ethan Hawke. "Hey," he said casually when I walked in, as though nothing much was different.

How we knew it was still our Manny was he was naked and pressed up against the bars of the crib and I could see his birthmark which I knew that there was no chance anyone else could have. Plus he didn't deny that he was our Emmanuel, he just said he now preferred the name Ethan Hawke, and I have to tell you if it hadn't been for the birthmark I would for sure have thought that the real Ethan Hawke had freaked out and come into our house and done something unspeakable with our beautiful baby. He admitted that he was our child, but told us he had just grown up quickly. He said we should have known that children in Los Angeles grow up quickly and maybe we should have thought of that when we decided to live there. (Even though we hadn't really decided to live there so much as ended up there when Sam got a job as head carpenter on a historical restoration project. If it were only about money I'd have just as soon added some hours at my old job in the produce department at Meijer's back in Kalamazoo, but his work really meant something to him.)

Of course the first thing Sam and I did was pray to god about it because we had pretty much counted on a baby that would grow up the way they usually do rather than in one big spurt like that. God sent us a message in the form of a perfectly heart-shaped cloud that we should just love and accept our child for who he was now, and that more would be revealed to us. Sam brought Ethan Hawke a flannel shirt and jeans from his closet but unfortunately his motor skills hadn't developed along with his body (surprisingly gaunt—this was obviously post-Uma/ *Before Sunset* Ethan Hawke), and although he could stand up, he had some trouble with his shirt buttons and couldn't get out of the crib at all, which was when I realized that he couldn't walk yet either. I slid the gate down and he almost fell right out of the crib, and seemed a little embarrassed when he realized he couldn't just brush it off and walk away. Manny had just learned to stand up before he turned into Ethan Hawke, and could take a few steps if you held both his hands, but it seemed obvious that Ethan Hawke was a little uncomfortable crawling downstairs, so Sam and I each took one of his hands and walked him down step by step and although he looked frustrated I could tell that inside he felt our unconditional love. Anyway, I knew he wasn't going to want the baby food I'd fixed him, but I'll tell you what, I was sure surprised when he asked if he could just have espresso! I told him we didn't have an espresso maker but that there was a Coffee Is Love a block down and I'd be happy to take him there after he ate some pancakes. It was obvious we were going to have to fatten him back up.

Maybe this goes without saying, but there are a lot of things you don't think about when your baby turns into a famous man overnight. He had the body and the vocabulary of an adult, but he was every bit as awkward as a baby. It took about twenty minutes to walk the two blocks, not just because he was learning to walk but because he would get distracted by stuff so easily; he'd take a few steps and seem like he was on a roll and then he'd see something move through the sky and he'd point and go, "Airplane!" and we'd get stalled for a few minutes while he contemplated the airplane even after it was well out of sight. A bunch of people followed us there with cameras and true to my baby Manny he stopped and smiled and waved for every one. When we finally made it to Coffee Is Love the espresso didn't really agree with him and he got a pained look on his face because he realized he was wearing big boy pants but that he was a ways away from graduating from his Nappies, and I was about to take him to the bathroom when this girl came over and asked if he'd sign a copy of his book (my son wrote a book—who knew?). I could tell he was trying really hard to hold it in and be friendly but to make matters worse he could not get a good grip on her pen and of course couldn't do anything but make a scribble. I apologized for his handwriting but she seemed not to care, and I walked him to the men's room but he looked totally scared to go in by himself. I thought it was because he couldn't walk without holding onto the wall, but he said quietly, "I need help." I told him I couldn't go in there with him so he did go in by himself, but he was in there for a good fifteen minutes and when he finally came out he had a little bit of pee on his pants and didn't want to leave until it dried. I promised him it didn't show and that I'd get him some Thick Pants later.

When we got home we had forty-three messages on the machine.

Ten of them were from various tabloids asking who the older woman was that he was seen holding hands with at Coffee Is Love, there were several from girls who seemed miffed not to have heard from him recently, four were from either Uma or her nanny asking when he was coming to pick up the kids, and a dozen were from some guy named Barry who wanted to know why he missed the junk in New York over the weekend ("Junket," Ethan Hawke corrected us, and Sam and I nodded blankly because we still had no idea what it was that he'd missed). Ethan Hawke looked stressed, which is not a look a baby should have in his wardrobe of looks, and curled into my lap with his head on my shoulder as though he didn't weigh a hundred and forty pounds. I hesitated for a second, but rocked him like he always liked, and he quickly fell asleep. You can imagine it was probably pretty exhausting to suddenly have a giant body and a fully formed personality if your day was previously filled with climbing socks.

Sam and I called an urgent meeting with our minister that evening because having an adult child was one thing and becoming grandparents in the same day was entirely another.

"God never gives you more than you can handle," he told us.

"It seems like he does," I said.

"But he doesn't," the minister said, and sent us on our way.

Not knowing what to do next, we asked Ethan Hawke what he wanted us to do. He said he did want to see his kids at some point but that movies didn't seem that important to him anymore and what he really wanted was just to have a normal childhood. He seemed so earnest and anyway we knew we didn't really have a choice.

We got him a big boy bed right away and we read to him every night.

Uma dropped off the kids several days later for the weekend and as a side note I was very impressed that she didn't come in a limo or even an SUV or a hybrid car which Ethan Hawke told me is like the reverse prestige car for reverse prestigious-minded celebrities. He held onto the door for balance when the kids came in and no one seemed to notice that anything was different. Well, his kids did later, of course, and actually you know how kids are, we explained to them that Daddy was kind of a baby now, and they were all too eager to help change his Thick Pants and play blocks with him. You could see he was conflicted about it, because he was so happy to see them, and I could also sort of tell that there was a part of him that was enjoying being on their level, but you know, he was used to picking them up and reading to them and even though he put on a good show for their sake, his angst was palpable when his four-year-old daughter read him *Goodnight, Moon* and he caught himself sucking his thumb as he was about to nod off.

Things got a little better when he started to walk on his own. One day he ventured out to Coffee Is Love without me, but I learned the hard way that although he could pass as an adult if you weren't paying close attention, he was still very much our little Manny in every other way, and I didn't find out the reason why he didn't go back for a long time after that until the following week when we were in line at Ralph's and I saw him on the front cover of *The Lightning Bolt*, flat on his bony butt on the sidewalk wailing like, well, a baby. I said, "Oh, pumpkin, did you fall down?" And he burst into tears right there in the supermarket like he was reliving the whole awful moment all over again. I put his head against my breast but quickly drew back for fear of photographers and just rubbed his head instead. He told me someone had helped him up and he had gone on to get his coffee anyway, but that he didn't stay long after realizing that coffee wasn't the same without the *Times* crossword. He was enjoying a stray copy of *Highlights for Children* (there had been a particularly raucous "Goofus and Gallant" in this issue, he told me) when he ran into Janeane Garofalo, who seemed doubtful that he was just checking it out for his kids.

He was excited about starting preschool, but that was not going to be possible, so we decided on homeschooling and he was an eager and quick learner. Within months he was reading Maurice Sendak to us and not long after that he had read all the Lemony Snicket books. Unfortunately his hunger to read led him to more sophisticated literature that he was obviously not mentally prepared for. One time we discovered him quietly weeping in the living room with a copy of *White Noise* in his lap. "Are we all going to die?" he asked.

How do you answer this question? Our faith teaches us that the kingdom of heaven is totally the ultimate awesome place, but should we expect our little baby to understand that just because he looks like a grown-up? Plenty of grown-up grown-ups can't handle that information. To be totally honest I have to count myself among them. I for sure don't believe all that devil stuff, but what if the kingdom of heaven is a skateboard park and the skate rats are totally stoked and my mom is sitting on the edge of the bowl with her knee pads on, despairing? You know, eternally? Or what if the kingdom of heaven plays Beethoven and Mahler 24/7 and my mother is finally at rest but Jimi Hendrix is just wigging for all endless ever? I was involved in thinking through a long list of permutations of this idea when Sam jumped in and said, "Hopefully not for a long time"—I suspect he may have perceived my thought process—"but it's nothing to be afraid of. Mommy and I believe in the promise of eternal life, which rocks it."

"Well..." Ethan Hawke said, thinking it through, "wouldn't it be better to be dead now, then?"

Probably we shouldn't have hesitated for quite so long before saying no on that one. We had to explain that we were here in our earthly lives for a reason, and of course he wanted to know what the reason was, and we said to do the will of god, and he said how do you know what that is, and we said we pray and listen for answers, and he said how do you know it's god talking, and we said that we always tried to be mindful of anything that might be the word of god, since we know that he doesn't just come walking up and ringing your doorbell but that on any given day there could be dozens of moments that maybe seemed like they were only coincidental, or even ordinary moments you might not think twice about, that could come in any form, like let's say Sam's in a super hurry to get to work on time and the light suddenly turns yellow—well of course everyone knows that yellow means slow down, but how many people take the time to really consider that on a deeper level? Or let's say you're thinking, oh, it might be a really good idea to hang up on this telemarketer right now seeing as how my doorbell's ringing and my toast is burning but then for "some reason" you hang on just long enough to find out they're from Angelo's Home Security System, get it, Angel-O? What then? We admitted that once in a while we weren't so sure, like the time we invested in the HP Cozy Company pretty much just on the basis of how its name struck us as unable to fail, and even when we found out what the products were—custom-made "cozies" for anything you might want to cover up—we thought that just sweetened the deal, but no, it turns out. Usually we feel pretty good that it's god's will even without a sign if it's like, something nice, like making ravioli for your crabby crab neighbor Mr. Downtree when his wife dies even though he moves your trash cans week after week because he says they're in his driveway which they obviously aren't and that it's not god talking if it's something like telling one and the same crab Downtree to go shoot himself even though it seems like the right thing in your own head when you back over your own trash cans smushing them beyond use because that's where he left them. I'm not sure if any of this helped Ethan Hawke or if it confused him more, but in any case we told him he had to stick to young adult books from now on even though he told us he didn't feel challenged.

He completed all of the homeschool work for grade levels 1-8 within a year and begged to go to a public high school. "Come on, Mom and Dad, I just want to hang with people my own age."

This was understandable, but "people my own age" was a phrase that seemed to have lost all meaning. We knew that he would be recognized in an ordinary high school and that there were all sorts of potential problems that an ordinary teenager might not have, but we also knew that he desperately needed socialization and that spending all his time with us, as nurturing as we tried to be, could only lead to intense psychotherapy down the road.

He enrolled in Beverly Hills High School explaining that he had never graduated and was eager to go to college one day. They urged him to get a GED, but he lied and said he wanted to know what he had missed and that he wanted to be treated just like everyone else.

This is where things started to turn to suck. I'm sorry to

have to use such a strong word, but I don't know how else to convey the downturn in events from this point forward.

Ethan Hawke came home from Coffee Is Love one Saturday afternoon and announced that he was in love with a barista named Agnès (pronounced Ohn-Yes) and at first we were very very happy for him because young love is a wonderful thing. We asked him to tell us all about her. He said, "She has shiny hair." Sam nodded and put his arm around Ethan Hawke as though this were the only reason one might fall in love except for I knew it wasn't because if there's one thing my hair isn't, it's shiny. I told Sam this might be a good time for him to talk some things over with our son and so they went out to the backyard but when they came back in I could tell it was too late. Ethan Hawke had told him that he already knew about sexual relations, and having two kids and all, I guess we should have known, but we still thought of him as our Manny and that our Manny would wait until he got married so that he would have god's blessing even though we hadn't. He told Sam that he was going to wait until he got married but that he had gotten a sign at the coffee shop in the form of the daily special which was a South American blend since he was an American from the south and the daily special had the word *blend* in it, written in two different colored chalks, top and bottom, in wavy "blending" kind of letters which he felt he could interpret no other way but that the two of them should blend in god's beautiful gift of lovemaking. That plus her name having Yes in it made him completely certain.

Ethan Hawke didn't think to mention that Agnès was only seventeen and although they did seem to be truly in love her father seemed to be truly in love with the idea of Ethan Hawke making him very very rich, so he came up with the idea of selling their pictures to *The Lightning Bolt* for $19,000 (which would maybe buy him a used SUV but unless he moves to a Third World country I wouldn't call this very rich) and for this price our little boy was immediately charged with statutory rape. He was only in jail for one night before we could raise the money to bail him out but one night in jail is way too many for any son of mine and he had a blackened eye when we brought him home and although he would not tell us what happened I could tell it was his "cellie" because the cellie was smiling in this super creepy way when they let our baby out, so before we left I went right over to the creepy cellmate and whispered to him with all of my utter truth, "Hurt my son again and I will bash you with a rock." I had a rather vivid image in my head as I spoke, of exactly how I would do it, over and over until the hateful mind that made him do such a thing was nothing as much as a stain on the floor, assuring me there was no chance this man would come out of his coma to harm another mother's child. I wanted to commit the sin of killing which I know is very against god's will and I usually try not to think violent thoughts but there are times like these when they just come.

Of course, Ethan Hawke had doubts about god after this. He was only in love but you know how your first love is, you tend not to use your noggin, so he somehow saw the whole thing as meaning that god was either bad and sending the hateful cellie to kick him in the eye, or worse, that he was not there at all. We told him that god does not kick good boys in the eye and that although we had to admit it sometimes seemed like god was not there (like if we thought too much about world hunger or all the bad sicknesses like typhoid or diphtheria or Parkinson's or about the men who sleep in the park or inconvenient truths or megastores that employ preschoolers in Taiwan for thirty cents an hour or about god taking so many of our parents away and stuff—at these times we just prayed harder not to think so much), we knew for sure that he was no matter what because he had sent my boy to my aged womb and there was almost no bigger miracle as far as we were concerned except for maybe the Mary thing.

We said many prayers together and stood by our baby through the whole awful trial where they made it out like he was as bad as OJ Simpson, we stood by our baby when Agnès broke it off with him because she didn't like the attention, and we stood by our baby when it seemed like for sure he was going to be convicted when the jury was deadlocked for seven days and finally ended in a mistrial. Then Agnès' father, who was also involved in a phony slip-and-fall case (which is where you supposedly slip and fall due to the negligence of someone but it is really just you putting a neck brace on and pretending like you're in pain), was found guilty of not really slipping and falling, casting quite a bit of doubt on his charges against our Manny. More than that, our Manny ended up sharing his story of heartbreak on *The Montel Williams Show*, at which time Patrick Dempsey and Charlotte Rampling both reached out to him admitting that they too had grown up quickly and, because of our baby, felt less alone, proving to us and to Ethan Hawke that everything really does happen for a reason. We never doubted.

VARIETIES OF LOUDNESS IN CHICAGO

PAOLO PAGANO, JR. ASPIRES TO BE LOUDER. It runs in the family. Little Paulie, as he's known, is the loudest. Loudness is to this family what college is to others. It's their pride, and it's what they're good at.

Jennie Watson is almost as loud.

Paulie Pagano and Jennie Watson live approximately one hundred yards apart, separated by one building, one alley, a universe, and you.

The stabbing couple, two porches down, is close behind, but that's a story for later.

Jennie lives in the new condo across the street, a warehouse rehabbed into *a unique urban loft-style experience*. Paulie lives behind you in a single-family home with his mother, who has, in her small parcel of land, an impressive vegetable garden. You won't be invited anytime soon, them not really knowing who you are, but you guess that a meal with the Paganos would be both interesting and delicious. You have never seen Paulie's mother smile, and suspect that it's been a long time. When she talks to the neighbors (a group with a surprising number of tenants and who show some indications of being one family, although after several years of observation, you're still not sure), they connect by complaining over the fence. *My back*, Paulie's mother will say in her thick Italian accent. *The weather. My son.* The neighbors nod solemnly. They know about backs and weather and sons. *Your tomatoes are gorgeous,* they will say. These are people who traded in their grass for cement. *Too much trouble*, they had told Paulie's mother, who nodded solemnly. Miscellaneous other people are also in apparent residence at the Paganos. These might include his sister, a girl who looks like his sister, and a heavyset guy who might be a cousin, but they're all frequently seen in the adjacent yard, so you can't be sure what sister belongs to which house. The girls who might be his sisters are also given toward loudness, although they aren't as ubiquitous outside and therefore appear somewhat less invested in their loudness than their possible brother. The girls who might be his sisters look just like Paulie, except they wear their hair in tight, shiny ponytails. These ponytails look like they could only hurt.

Jennie, in any case, likely has no such aspirations of loudness. She just is.

Little Paulie is twenty-three years old. When you moved in, he was seventeen and already bald. Upon hearing the news of his being a teenager, you spent some time examining him from your porch window whenever possible, trying to process this information, trying to understand how a seventeen-year-old anywhere could pass for forty, trying to understand what in seventeen years adds up to bald and forty-looking. You will come to know that possibilities include a dead dad and a close association with a bunch of local gangbangers, also loud, and who have no interest whatsoever in Paulie's front door, or any parts on or adjacent to it that might ring in a pleasant way, a way that only its occupants might hear. When they want to see Paulie, they come through the alley and they yell, *Paul-ee. Paul-ee!* Paulie never comes on the first eight or nine Paulies. Usually his mother will intervene with a few more Paulies, a final loud *Paolo!* and some words in Italian. She is a small, square woman, but you sense that she can and has and will again hit him and it will hurt. Little Paulie has one expression. It's a scowl.

Jennie, blond, is twenty-six, a size two, and owns a clothing business and her condo, directly across from your front window. How you know this is she spends a good deal of time on her balcony (actually, what this is is more or less a railing in front of a set of sliding doors, with a plank just wide enough for one Jennie-sized person to stand on) talking on the phone and telling people these things. Jennie used to be a size zero, but then she started working out. So she didn't, *like, gain weight or anything,* her body *just totally changed which is a total bummer because I had like four pairs of Chip and Peppers and now I can't wear them at all* Chip and Peppers are jeans that cost two hundred dollars. How you know this is she told the person she was talking to, who didn't know either. Jennie has several expressions, but they're all in the ballpark of overstimulated.

Paulie's interests include sitting on the roof of his garage, cars from the late '70s/early '80s, motorcycles, dogs, tattoos, rap, weed, and the sound of his own name. He also seems to like being perceived as someone who's always "around" and knows what's going on. Not in the world, but around. Sometimes these interests are combined in various ways to produce greater loudness. You suppose he wishes his dog were louder, but he's not much of a barker. Once he even tried to lick your hand, but Paulie yanked him back, clearly disappointed with the friendliness of his pit bull. Sometimes an afternoon will include a combination of rap, played from the car, parked in the alley but running, weed, and some of the guys on the roof of his garage. On these days you stay off the porch. Paulie could and might pass you the joint from there. It would be uncomfortable.

Jennie's interests include Jennie. Or talking about Jennie. Boys and fashion, occasionally, but only as they pertain to Jennie. She's the kind of girl who will stop you in the middle of a story and say, *That reminds me*, and tell you a story about herself that has nothing to do with your story in any way you can discern. Your story could be about your sick aunt which will remind her of her aunt which will remind her of something about herself and your sick aunt will be no part of it.

When you first moved in, you could tell it was summer when the scent of night-blooming jasmine filled the air and the neighborhood kids started shooting. The storage warehouse across the street was largely quiet except on nights when the neighborhood kids hung around, sometimes with babies in tow, fighting about who'd been in the neighborhood longer— interesting in no small part due to the fact that the people fighting about this topic were barely fourteen. In spite of her own short time there, Jennie has her own proprietary feelings about her corner of the street. She will talk to anyone who is moving in, looking in, and, it seems, merely walking by, and tell them that she was the first one to move in. You have the sense that in a certain way she believes she's pioneered the very concept of moving. What interests you here is that every word uttered by Jennie is distinctly audible but never can you hear the person she's talking to. Or, at. You have the sense that Jennie thinks of herself and her living here as *edgy*. Whatever this means, though, she isn't. You aren't even edgy, and you were here before the condos came. You live here because it's cheap, but it's worth noting that you feel at ease here in a way you never do on the Gold Coast. On the Gold Coast you feel like an impostor.

The summer Jennie moves in is also the summer of the motorcycle. Little Paulie gets a bike and rides it often but always comes back within ten minutes. You are fairly sure that Paulie removed the muffler upon purchase, and that he comes back quickly because he will not go farther than can be heard in his own 'hood— there would be no point if his loudness were heard only by strangers. Kind of like if a tree falls in the forest, if the tree cares whether or not the forest hears it make a sound. You believe that if for some reason his license were revoked, Paulie would be just as happy to gun the bike in back of his house. You have seen him ride from the alley to the corner deli, which might be twenty paces from his front door. But as you know, Paulie does not use the front door in any capacity—answering,

entering, or exiting—and perhaps Paulie is thinking that someone will think he came from somewhere else.

Jennie walks to the deli, but prefers to hold her fights in
the street. For a while, she has a boyfriend. He has highlights in
his flat-ironed hair. This isn't what they fight about. This is what
they have in common. What they fight about is him not paying
enough attention to her feelings. *How could you not know that my
ex–best friend wore that horrible perfume and that it would bring back
terrible feelings?* Jennie has her arms spread wide and her head
forward. If she weren't a size two it might be a threatening posture. What it seems like coming from Jennie is something she
saw someone do on that *Laguna Beach* show. *It was a gift! I can't
read your fucking mind!* he shouts. *And I'm sick of fucking trying.
I never asked you to!* Jennie yells. *I told you what I wanted! Okay,*
he says, *then I'm sick of you. And I'm gone. Whatever!* she shouts,
turning back to her apartment. You sense that she can and has
and will again, if he comes back, hit him. Fights like this tend to
take place after you've gone to bed but are worth getting up for.
Sometimes you even go watch the show with your downstairs
neighbor. He's always up late. Later, you will find out that Jennie
and her boyfriend have broken up five times already since they
met three months prior. *I'm so sure he'll be back,* she says, having
wasted no time getting on the phone. You're so sure that if he
does, she will hit him. But it won't hurt, which will only make
him look like more of a wuss.

Rumors have gone around about Paolo Pagano, Senior,
that he was a small-time mob guy, that he was rubbed out or
whacked or whatever they say, but that Little Paulie didn't show

a lot of promise in the area of Mafia, and so was overlooked when the time came to promote. Paulie compensates for this by going to jail anyway. You will never know why for sure, you will only know that this is the quietest summer ever on your block. You know only that one day when you hear a gunshot, you look out the front window, nothing, you look out the back window, nothing, you look out the side window into the alley and there are six police cars, Paulie in handcuffs, and Paulie's dead pit bull in a pool of blood. Later there will be a large tattoo of the dog's head on Paulie's left bicep, *RIP Damien II*. For a time there will be a shrine, prayer candles and flowers and a big rawhide bone, until the city puts a speed bump in the alley.

You were kind of getting used to the gunfire, but you hadn't yet seen it end with blood. It seemed to you like the gangbangers tended just to shoot, and that whether or not they hit anything wasn't the point. The cops, in this incident anyway, hit their target.

When Little Paulie comes back the following summer, he looks even older, if that's possible, and there's a new girl in the house who looks different enough from Paulie and his possible sisters to guess she's a girlfriend, confirmed a few months later with the birth of Little Little Paulie. When Paulie the third begins walking and talking, there is a spike in utterances of the name Paulie, which no doubt pleases the elder Little Paulie.

The summer Paulie comes back there's another new condo going up next to his house. The construction is on a loudness level comparable with Paulie and/or his transportation, and you can imagine that the loudness of construction vs. the loudness of one guy, if that were your source of pride, would be a drag. It displeases Paulie, and it displeases you too, both because you could do without more Jennies and because it's also the summer you get burglarized and you suspect no one notices at least partly because of the noise. But it pleases Jennie. *My property value has already doubled, practically! Someone down the hall sold their unit for twice what I paid!* You are sure the person she's talking to on the street is a casual acquaintance at best, if not a total stranger. You feel mildly uncomfortable thinking of an apartment as a unit. You tend not to think of your home as a unit. You are fairly sure that Paulie does not think about things like units and property value. You are fairly sure that Paulie was born in that house and will die in that house. Or near it. You are fairly sure you will leave when it's no longer cheap, which will be soon, and that more Jennies will follow. You don't know if this is good or bad.

You and Paulie acknowledge that you have seen one another, around, on more than one occasion with nods, the kind where your head goes up and back, where you lead with your chin. Once, he held your door when you found a sweet chair in the alley. After the burglary, you ask a few neighbors, including Paulie, if they happened to see anything. Paulie says no, but to let him know if you see anything again. *I know some people*, he says. You have a lot of thoughts about what this means. You secretly enjoy the idea that you know someone who knows some people who might do something very very bad on your behalf, even though you'd never ask. You are sure that Paulie does know some people. When anything happens in the 'hood, Paulie is on the scene. You have seen him at the site of more than one car accident, looking on. You have even seen him at the site of a car accident on the local news. You have seen him when the deli burned down and when the stabbing couple got taken away.

You try to avoid Jennie's side of the street, but she's seen you in the deli and you meet up in the cheese section at Whole Foods. You're carrying a hand basket containing a box of crackers and a wedge of Brie to bring to a potluck. Jennie has a cartful of everything and anything and when she sees you she greets you like an old friend and says, *Can you believe these prices OMG I'm totally going to max out my card hey I'm having a sample sale you should totally come here's a flyer.* You enjoy the idea of discount designer clothes, but feel no more comfortable about having Jennie on your side than you do about Paulie.

Little Little Paulie, about three when you finally move, shows early signs of carrying on the Pagano family legacy of loudness. He drives his Playskool car with one hand on the top of the wheel and the other hanging out of the window. He looks worried, serious, almost exactly like his dad, except cute. But so far, you haven't heard him make a sound.

BLUE GIRL

When I was four years old, the word BLUE appeared on my forehead in cerulean block-print letters. At the time I wasn't aware that this was anything out of the ordinary. I thought maybe my parents were trying to teach me how to read. My parents thought I had taught myself to write. *Oh, honey, yes, that is blue!* they said.

What's blue? I asked. I hadn't seen it yet.

Silly, they said. *On your head.*

I reached for my head. I didn't feel anything. They showed me a mirror. There were blue letters there. But I hadn't written them.

Show us how you write, honey, they said. *Can you spell the other colors? I bet you can spell red.* They handed me a box of crayons.

I knew my colors, and I could recite the alphabet and even copy my name, but I didn't know how to write. *Mommy, I didn't write it. Did you write it?*

Well of course I didn't write it, Jimmy, did you write it?

Why would I write on my daughter?

Just a question, Jim.

This conversation went on for a while and became somewhat heated and bizarre. There wasn't anyone else in the house. I had no siblings. Finally I said, *Maybe Bart wrote it.*

Bart was our cocker spaniel.

No, honey, Bart can't write.

They finally got tired of the debate. *Well, let's go wash it off and get you ready for school.*

It didn't wash off. Not with soap, not with shampoo, not when they scrubbed really hard, and not with any of the things they brought in from the kitchen, which included olive oil, lemon, and Clorox. My forehead was now cerulean with a very red background.

At school my parents apologized and told my teacher Miss Holly that I must have used a permanent marker. Miss Holly chuckled like it was no big deal, and said she'd seen stranger things, like when Bobby Millman put a button up his nose and when Debbie Ross came in with the right half of her hair cut off. Ironic, then, that those two would be the ones to start the chanting. *Blue Girl! Blue Girl! Blue Girl!*

It was shortly after that that it changed. Unbeknownst to me. It now said STEW. In a deep shade of pink.

Miss Holly brought me straight to the principal's office. My word changed to a burgundy DIRGE on the way there. She explained to the principal that I was misbehaving and causing the other children to be distracted. I spent several hours there.

DIRGE stuck for some time. The principal also tried to wash it off and I told them we already tried that at home. She sent me to the infirmary. The nurse rolled her eyes. *I can't do anything here*, she said. I was sent home and asked to remain there until something changed.

The only thing that changed, periodically, was the word.

On the first day it read LAMB (alabaster) and KNAVE (pistachio) and then back to BLUE again.

On the second day it said, in yellow of course, TAXI.

On the third day it alternated between OMELET and DETOUR, and on the fourth day it said LANGUID in gray and stayed that way for several more days until it changed to PUNK in black, and that's when my parents decided to take me to a doctor.

The doctor took many tests and pronounced me perfectly healthy. My head said MERGE. My parents took me to a specialist. I still don't know what he was a specialist in. The specialist nodded a lot and said *Hm* quite a few times and took more tests that were all inconclusive. He finally decided that it must be psychological, and referred us to a shrink.

Needless to say, more tests. Rorschachs that reminded me only of benign things like horses and butterflies and games involving pegs and holes and what do you think of when I say

Sky?

Blue.

Sun?

Moon.

Night?

Day.

All of which was also inconclusive until he finally said, *Well, there is one more thing*, and pulled a large book off the shelf and looked up Bigg-Stanley Syndrome, the description of which more or less fit. Something about moods and biochemical reactions and no known treatment. Still, he suggested eliminating all color from my diet (an unpleasant week of mashed potatoes and milk) and prescribed something, which resulted in a series of short stories printed on my head, which resulted in us going back to the shrink, who then said, *Yes, that is a possible side effect.*

Several shrinks and dubious treatments later, my parents decided to cut my hair into bangs, covering my forehead. This worked fine indoors, but once on the playground under moderately windy conditions, my words appeared again and so the torture resumed. *Mood Head*! is what they called me.

Finally we decided on a hat.

I transferred to a new preschool and it was explained to the administration that I was a special needs case and I was to be allowed to wear my hat in class at all times.

I didn't make a lot of friends. When I eventually got to fourth grade there was another kid with a hat. He had leukemia. We made friends. When he died, the other kids wanted to know why I hadn't also died. I told them I didn't have leukemia. *Then why*, they said, *do you wear a hat?* I told them I just needed to. A bully took my hat and saw the word KIMONO on my head.

I transferred twice more before my parents decided to homeschool.

Around tenth grade I started to miss being around other

kids my age, even mean ones, and decided to try going back again. I knew there were weirder kids than me in school. Kids who were weird on purpose. They chose a progressive school where they hoped I might be better accepted.

I went without a hat.

I was accepted.

They thought I was expressing myself. I let them think this. A boy named Eddy Forrest asked me to the movies. We smoked a joint and made out in his Dart in the parking lot and my word changed from ITCH to MARVEL right before his eyes. *Whoa, how did you do that?* he asked.

Do what, I said?

Change your head

You're stoned.

Seeeriously, he said, nodding.

I realized, at this time, that I was either going to have to get my dates stoned on a regular basis or think of a new plan.

I developed a mild marijuana habit.

But by the time I got to college I got tired of having to ditch all these guys before they figured out something really was up with my head.

I started telling people about Bigg-Stanley Syndrome. I became a champion for the little-known cause of Bigg-Stanley Syndrome. There were leaflets.

I got fewer dates.

I lost my virginity to a drunken half-back at a moment when my head happened to say GO TEAM.

Graduation was coming up and once again I had no plan.

Performance art seemed like an obvious possibility, but I felt like that would be cheating. I wasn't trying to make a statement. I had a condition. I was studying for a chem final in the quad when a guy came over and sat down next to me. He was cute but smelled like he hadn't showered in a week.

Hey, he said. I nodded. *I'm in your chem class,* he said. *You live in Franklin Hall, right?* I nodded.

By now I knew there was a small contingency of people who were into people with unusual conditions, like amputees and stuff. I did a fairly good job of avoiding them. Once I fooled around with a guy who seemed really nice on the first couple of dates, flowers, a tie even, pulling out chairs and all, but then when he was in my apartment one time he whispered in my ear, *I can love you, baby, I'll take care of you,* which, um, wasn't what I was looking for.

But chem class guy turned out to be okay, he was really the first one for whom my head was neither here nor there. I got him into the shower, if you know what I mean, and one day when he took my face in his hands, words appeared on his head. It said I WILL FALL IN LOVE WITH A FRENCH WOMAN AND MOVE INTO HER LOFT ON THE SEINE. He seemed to have no knowledge of this because the way he was looking at me quite adoringly contradicted the message on his head. Nevertheless, it was as clear a message as I'd ever seen on anyone's head—my own had always been so random—and I pushed him away and got out of the shower and into a towel. *What'd I do?* he asked. It had already started to fade when I took his hands off me, so I quickly showed him the mirror.

He was surprised to see such a message, of course, and didn't say anything for a minute, but finally he denied it. *I don't know any French woman. I love you.* He even started crying because he could tell that I was about to break up with him.

I knew in my bones that he was both sincere and that he would meet a French woman. *Get dressed,* I said.

We went down the hall and started knocking on doors. I asked the RA to put her hands on my face. Her head said I WILL ENTER A GRADUATE PROGRAM IN SOCIAL WORK AND MARRY A CLIENT.

I grabbed a guy in the study lounge who was nodding out with a bowl of chips on his lap in front of *Wheel of Fortune*. REHAB 5X was all it said. The guy next to him read RICH WIFE.

See? I said to my boyfriend.

What does that prove? It just means you can make your words show up on other people.

I don't think so. Take a better look at rehab guy.

A dark-haired girl who had been watching came over. *Do me,* she said. She had a faint accent I couldn't place with just the two words.

I put her hands on my face.

I WILL TAKE YOUR BOYFRIEND TO MY HOMELAND, it said. I looked at my boyfriend. Guilty.

I was somewhat disappointed about the loss, but as I said, I'd had no plan until then.

I got one of the guys from computer lab to build me a website. I taped a commercial and bought some cheap airtime on the local cable channels in the middle of the night.

1-800-MOOD-HED. I tried not to overdo it like Miss Cleo. I just gave a brief demonstration and said, *Call or whatever*.

I could not take all the calls. I gathered pretty quickly that Miss Cleo must not have been working on her own. Of course, I had to meet the people in person, and even though the readings were quick, I could not meet the demand, and I tried to hire out, but only one other Bigg-Stanley guy showed up and he didn't have the gift. His readings produced nothing but smiley faces and the occasional four-leaf clover. Nevertheless, I had quite a career on my hands.

I quickly amassed a huge fortune. I bought a beautiful home on the beach. I was on magazine covers and I was consulted by presidents. There were attempts at exposés, but every single one of them was convinced after I read their own heads. Even the ones who were uncertain about their readings were easily convinced that it wasn't a trick.

My love life still sucked.

On the book tour, a guy in a baseball hat came up to the podium. I reached across the table to sign his book but he didn't have one. He took off his hat.

He had Polaroids on his forehead. White border, color Polaroid pictures in the same place as the words were on me.

They changed a couple of times while we talked. I guessed that some of them were from his childhood. He told me that they were often random, with pictures of people he didn't know at all appearing occasionally. I asked if he would put his hands on my face. Granted, I was curious to see what would happen, but he was also pretty cute. He said he was hoping I'd ask.

I saw a slide show of works by great artists, mostly still lifes; sunflowers by Van Gogh, some Wayne Thiebaud cakes, and *Still Life with Biscuits* by Picasso. It was a nice show, but it didn't give us anything concrete. I don't know that much about art so any ideas I could have come up with about it were subject to interpretation.

Still, it was worth a conversation. I like biscuits.

YOU MUST BE THIS HAPPY TO ENTER

WHAT HAPPENED WAS I WAS at yet another dreadful opening when some dude in those kind of architect glasses said to me something like, "That which doesn't provoke has no meaning," and, you know, first of all, who talks like that—"That which"— nobody is who, and second of all, well, it just burned me. It's not irrelevant that the show that night was by this artist who does these giant installations of Barbie war scenes, with, like, hundreds of Barbies with their hair all chopped off, dressed in camouflage and carrying machine guns; dead and wounded Barbies all over with their very lifelike guts spilling out, and Kens tending to the victims dressed in those old-timey white nurse costumes with the little red crosses on them but with short pants and cutoff sleeves. I've stopped trying to figure out what people like this are even trying to say because I'm not trying to hear it. I don't care if you think the only thing worth depicting in your art is a soulless, violent, war-torn world. I don't care, Mr. Gallery Glasses

Guy, for the long-winded, thesaurus-y explanation about why the lone pencil mark Joe Grad-student left on your wall is a brilliant denouncement of beauty in art. I don't understand why it has to be hard and sad and bad for it to be deep. We've all had our hard sad badnesses in life, and I just thought, would it be so wrong for art to be about something happy? It's a legitimate feeling.

So, I think you can see that this was where the bells went off for me and right then I decided to do something about it. I started my own gallery and I made a giant sculpture to go out front so that you know before you even go in what the deal is. I'm primarily a photographer, but in this case I wanted something really eye-catching to make my point and draw people in. Remember those little figurines of babies from Spencer Gifts or wherever that said, *I love you this much*, with the arms open wide? This statue is like a giant version of that except it says, *You must be this happy to enter*. For the opening I went to great lengths to create work that was, as I saw it, not about anything besides the true joy of life. In the window I hung a photo I'd taken of this woman totally laughing—no doubt because she's eating ice cream, but she's super thin and from what I can see rich, and she's out shopping, and why shouldn't she be happy?

Inside I hung many other photos of people being happy. On one wall I hung what I call the happy series: *Happy Dude*, *Happy Dude Wearing Shades*, *Happy Chick*, and *Happy Chick with Rainbow [Thinking about Unicorns]* (for real—you could see the rainbow but I could tell there was another layer to her happiness so I asked her and suggested the longer title). Plus also: *Happy Family*, *Happy Baby Numbers 1-6* (there are a lot of happy babies out there and I think some of us could take a lesson from them), plus also *Happy Waving Abraham and Silas, Ten Months* (twins who have a very positive outlook in spite of their origin of smallness). On another wall I hung the love series: *Love Rocks, Love Totally Rocks, Love Rocks It Hard,* and *Sheep Love* (that's between sheep—it's a photo of sheep who are only just nuzzling in a loving way—not people and sheep; that is not love, that's just a bad website). On a third wall I hung the sunshine series: *Sunshine in the Bronx, Sunshine in Seattle* (because people don't think the sun shines there so much, but when it does people are exceptionally happy), *Sunshine on Division Street, Sunshine in Dresden,* and so on.

The opening got quite a turnout, but let me tell you I was sure surprised at what ended up going down. There I was discussing my passion for happiness over a glass of wine when suddenly six police officers burst in and charged me with— well, they said I didn't take the photo in the window and that they suspected I had not taken many of the others, and they arrested me and took me in to the police station and finger- printed me and everything. I assured them that I absolutely did take that photo as well as all the others and they said it was impossible for me to have taken the photo in the window, which was according to them a very famous photograph taken by some old dude named Gary Wino-something, and they at- tempted to verify this by pointing out that according to my driver's license I was only twenty-three years old and therefore not even a thought in my mother's head at the time of the taking of the photo.

I said, Um, I guess you guys haven't heard of something called *time travel*?

This was funny to them. Ha ha ha, the police squad laughed, that's funny.

I said I wasn't surprised that there was a similar photograph out there, because there had been a number of people taking photos of this woman. Everyone had agreed she was unusually happy and that it was a moment that should be documented.

Young lady, they said, clearly under obligation to use phrases like this, as policemen, Young lady, they said again, time travel? Is not real. Wouldn't you just split right now if it were?

Yes, I said, I just might, but I don't have any of my stuff. It's not just like, Oh, I think I'd like to go to 1986 right now, *poof.* It's an effort.

Oh, of course. Well, here's a nice cell for you until someone comes from the future to bail you out. Ha ha ha.

They put me in a temporary cell with this guy about my age who did not look like he could be guilty of anything besides being extremely foxy.

Hey, the foxy dude said to me, they bring you in for being happy too?

This is probably the part where most people would say, *Whaaaaa?* but where I, being me, would and did say, I think they did!

Yeah, it's no longer legal in three states, he said. I bet you didn't know that.

No way, I said. We have to move as soon as we get out!

Seriously, he said. Unfortunately the jail term is open-ended. You don't get out until you understand the true pain of life again.

I said, Nuh uh!

He said, Yuh huh.

We'll have to fake it, I said.

Forget it. I'm incapable. He shrugged, like even jail wasn't going to make him sad, like it was only a minor inconvenience.

You can't pretend? I said.

I don't think so, he said.

What if you try thinking of something really sad?

I can't really think of anything.

Your parents still alive?

Happy and healthy. And rich.

Married?

Yeah, he said *almost* sadly.

Did you ever lose a pet?

My gerbil had the sniffles one time. We were a little worried, but he was fine.

What about the state of the world?

I know, that's bad. But in my missionary work I found so much beauty among even the poorest people that I can't really muster it up. Did you know that a lot of disadvantaged people around the world have such a strong faith in god that they really don't feel sorry for themselves? I met this one girl in Costa Rica who gave her only pair of broken sandals to an old woman because she had none at all. Jesus will carry me, she said. That kind of thing makes me weep all the time. But for joy.

He was a *missionary*. A foxy young happy missionary! Who

wept for joy! I knew right then that I was going to have to find a way to break out. I asked him one last question I thought was a guarantee.

Okay, look, everyone's had their heart broken once at least. It's like the doctors should just whisper this in your tiny baby ears when they hand you over to your mom: All we know for sure is your heart will break, and god bless. You have to have had your heart broken.

Not yet, he smiled at me.

That sealed it. Listen, I said, leaning in, I can get us out of here. You've time traveled before, right?

No way, man, that's dangerous shit, he said.

No, it's only dangerous if you stay somewhere for more than an hour. That's when the time-space continuum starts to get warped and the future starts changing in weird ways.

What's the point of time traveling at all if you don't want to change the future?

I had never thought about that.

Huh, I said. I guess I didn't want to be responsible. What if I set off a volcano somehow and wiped out a whole civilization?

What if you adopted a crack baby who grew up to be the president? A good president, he added quickly, sensing where my mind was going. The best president ever.

Couldn't I just do that now? I asked.

Well, yeah, I think you could, he smiled.

He was looking so damn foxy right then I just about died, but as much as I wanted to raise sixteen homeless babies with him, I wasn't convinced that raising the presidential crack baby in jail would work out completely well, so I said, Look, I need to get a bunch of stuff from home but I'll be back.

I started thinking about as many sad things as hard as I could. It was very difficult, because I really am the kind of person, just like him, who sees beauty in even the darkest places. A lot of my happy photos are from places where you don't expect to see a lot of happiness. The Division Street photo was taken during a time when it was just nothing but drunks in bars, like if I'd taken it at night it would have been all super *Days of Wine and Roses* or whatever with the neon sign–montage kind of thing going on over the drunk's head as he stumbled home trying to remember where or who he even was but since I took it during the day I happened to catch a bunch of old guys playing cards on a stoop with the sun shining off the backs of the cards and this one was wiping his eyes he was laughing so hard and for all I know they could've all been drunk that whole day and every day before it, but nevertheless I found it to be of a unique and spectacular beauty. I took the Dresden picture right after the war—this little girl had been crying because she just lost her mom (I knew this because one of the awesome bonuses of time travel is that you can suddenly speak fluent—whatever they speak in Dresden or wherever), anyway, she found her favorite doll in the rubble of her house and was just giggling when I took the picture.

Not to get sidetracked but I think the reason I'm so personally happy is that I too believe hard in god's will and although I do not have the first idea why things happen like they do, I find myself generally untroubled knowing that god is looking down on all of us totally all of the time. I know that bad bad bad things happen with alarming frequency, but I believe that very often good things happen because of bad things, and I would almost argue that in my experience more good things happen because of bad things, because if things were mostly good all the time, why would anyone try very hard to make them better? Whereas if things are mostly bad, I think people are sort of forced to rise up to their best selves. I don't know if that makes sense and maybe it's super Deepak Chopra or whatever, but it's what I think.

Anyway, that said, I was trying to get us out, so I was sitting there thinking about conventionally sad things: war and poverty and corporate greed and terrible diseases and hurricanes and all that and, trust me, I came as near to crying as I ever have when I thought about the president being reelected, but none of it was working until I thought of my future husband the foxy young missionary and what if we had to get married in jail and pee in front of other people for the rest of our lives and raise our babies in there because we were too happy to get out? Then I started imagining the beautiful lives we never had, with no simple ceremony on the beach, no cute owl mugs from the '70s, no barbecues in the yard, no chocolate chip pancakes on Sunday, no new school shoes or three-ring binders, no taking the kids camping or having a spiritual experience at the Grand Canyon, no "No you may certainly not have ruby-encrusted high-tops just because all the kids have them," no grounding them when they've snuck out to go see their delinquent boyfriends, no su-per-8 movies of them graduating from pre-K or eighth grade or medical school, no wrapping up together in Grandma's love-holey afghan on a freezing night in September already, no taking in our parents when they're old and shaky—no nothing normal at all ever even, and finally I was crying so hard it felt like I was convulsing with the pain of the whole world, and, of course, as soon as he noticed, a policeman came right over and unlocked the door. He said, I can see you understand the true pain of life now, try not to forget it.

I won't, I won't, I said, wiping my tears and whispering, I'll be right back, to my new boyfriend.

I went home and filled my knapsack with provisions for return. I put on my fuzzy slippers, ate three Drake's fruit pies, clapped four times, and said, County jail, cellblock 1, May 25, 2004, 7:45:33 p.m. You can't take chances with the time thing, for obvious reasons. Three seconds off and you might find yourself in a cellblock with some kind of violent criminal instead of your hot missionary. Anyway, so I went back to the jail only to encounter a new problem. He didn't want to go. I didn't figure we had a long time for discussion about it with the police guards right there. He said he was too happy. I named a whole bunch of other times and places where he could be even happier. I said we could go all the way back to Eden if he wanted to and I'd promise to stay away from apples. He said he was happy enough and that he thought he could do some good right where he was. I was getting really discouraged and then he finally said, I think god put me here for a reason. You know I couldn't argue with that so I said, Well, do you think that god put me here too? And he said, I for sure do think that. I knew then that he was my soul mate and that homeless babies or not we'd just have to rise up.

THE MOST EVERYTHING IN THE WORLD

LAST NIGHT MY HUSBAND ASKED ME, If you lived on a desert island and could only bring three things, what would you bring, and I said, I'd bring pen and paper and you. He said if he could bring only three things he'd bring pen and paper and cheese. I asked him why he wouldn't bring me, and he said he didn't think of me as a thing, plus he knew I was already there. I said, Well, I don't think of you as a thing either, but I wouldn't want to be on a desert island without you. Anyway, if you know I have pen and paper already, wouldn't you bring something else? He said, Good point, and then said he wasn't so sure about the pen and paper anyway, because he could probably draw in the sand, or on some bark or something. So I guess I'd bring bread and cheese and wine, he said. But we don't drink, I said. He said, I think if we were on a desert island we might want to start. I wonder, though, if we couldn't make cheese and wine on the desert island, I said. Well, we probably wouldn't know in advance if there were grapes and milk available. I think I'd like to bring a lot of clothes, I said. Those people on that TV show are only there for thirty-nine days at most and they start looking really grungy by the end of the first week. Yeah, but who cares, my husband said. We could just go naked always. I dunno, I'm not that into being naked, I said. But I'm into you being naked, he said. What if it gets cold, I said. I'll build you a nice hut, he said. Okay, maybe I could go naked if we had bug spray. And sunscreen. I don't think I'd look so sexy naked, sunburnt, and covered in bug bites. If you were sunburnt you might not notice the bug bites, he said. If I were sunburnt I might get melanoma, I said. Look at it this way, though, if we moved to a desert island, my husband said, we wouldn't have to worry about health insurance. No, I said, we'd only have to worry about health. But we worry about that anyway. This way there's one less worry, he said. Okay, but I still don't want melanoma. You could sit in the shade. Yes, but what if I got eaten by a wild animal while I was sitting in the shade trying not to get melanoma? Some weird cross between a warthog and a mountain lion, I said. I don't think health insurance would do us much good if that happened, he said. A doctor might, I said. But there probably wouldn't be a doctor on the desert island, I guess. These are the chances we have to take, he said. So if I have you right, that if some warthog mountain lion eats my legs off and I don't happen to die, what then? Then that's what's meant to be, he said. We can take comfort in knowing that we are not giving our money to the man. Look, I said, I don't like giving my money to the man any more than you do, but I'm the one lying here with my legs eaten off. It's not like I'd be immune to the warthog mountain lion, my husband said. Or rare diseases that we've never even heard of, he added. You could be lying there with your legs eaten off and I could be unable to help you because my arms are paralyzed from Poison Mango Syndrome. And this would be better than having health insurance how? I asked. We would lead the only truly all-natural lifestyle anywhere on the planet; we would be accepting our fate, he said. In a lot of pain, I said. That's when the wine would come in handy, my husband said. I don't think wine is going to do it, I said. We could bring morphine, he said. You can't just get morphine, I said. In Mexico you can, he said. Maybe we should move to Mexico instead of a desert island, I said. But Mexico isn't deserted, my husband said. Yes, but I never wanted to move anywhere, I said. But a deserted island would be so awesome, he said. What if it got boring, I said. Don't you think we'd get bored after a while? On an island with warthog mountain lions? he asked. I'm thinking that after my legs get eaten off and your arms get paralyzed we may be limited in our activities. That's when the acid comes in handy, my husband said. Acid, I said. You know, or mushrooms, he said, whichever. Okay, so let me understand. We're half-immobile, possibly dying, and now we're tripping? No? he asks. What about if we had a spear, my husband said. To spear snakes with. How are you going to spear snakes with no arms? I asked. Let's say I still have arms in this scenario, he said. I don't think I can go to a desert island with snakes, I said. Well, snakes wouldn't be the only creepy thing on the island, I'm sure, he said. That's right,

I said. You're the one who gets so freaked out by spiders, I said. Ugh, I do hate spiders, he said. Spiders would probably be the *best* of the insects on the island. The spiders would be like our pets. Oh, my husband said. You know what, though, I said, if we're in charge of this whole desert island thing, couldn't we design the island too? A bug-free island? Yes, he said, we can. No bugs no warthog mountain lions for us, he said. Only beautiful flowers and fruit and vegetables and cotton, I said. Flora and fauna. What exactly is fauna? my husband asked. I don't know, I picture deer, I said. Me too! he said. That's so weird. But deer have ticks which have lyme disease, I said. And they eat your vegetables. Okay, so no fauna. Only flora, he said. And sheep, I said. Are sheep fauna? I don't know. But if we had sheep we could have milk and cheese and wool. And lamb, he said. I could never kill a sheep, I said. They're so cute. No, he said, they have weird alien eyes. I could kill a sheep. Okay, I said, but not in the hut. Not anywhere near the hut. Or me. No sheep killing near the hut, got it. Okay, so no bugs. Fruit, vegetables, cotton, sheep. Maybe we should consider bringing a farmer. I don't want to go to a desert island to work so hard, I said. What if it just farms itself? If it grows exactly what we need. That would be awesome, I said. And it only ever gets cold enough so that it's nice sleeping weather, or to justify sitting by a fire on the beach. Yes, he said, but a fire is no good without marshmallows. If we bring marshmallows we have to bring chocolate and graham crackers, I said. That's very true. You know what else would be great, he said, is a table saw. I could do a lot with a table saw. You could bring a table saw and I could bring a sewing machine. We are going to need some hobbies. If you bring a sewing machine, he said, wouldn't you also have to bring a bunch of fabric? Yes, well, those would be my three things. And thread. That's four, he said. You're only bringing the table saw. Can you bring the thread for me? No, I just haven't picked my other thing yet. How about if we bring four things, then. Okay, I'm bringing the table saw, the bread and the wine and the cheese and paint. That's five. Crap. I need to rethink the sewing machine. Can I count a sewing kit as one thing? Sure, my husband said. (That's the kind of guy he is.) Okay, then. A sewing machine, a sewing kit, some fabric, and pen and paper for me. That's five, my husband said. But I need pen and paper, I said. Look, if no one's going to read it, what's the difference if you just think it? We don't know that no one's going to read it. Anyway, thinking isn't the same as writing. No? he asked. I had to think about this for a while. It got me a little dizzy. Okay, well, let's assume it is different, what if they discover our writings hundreds of years from now and we're held up as these pioneers, able to sustain ourselves with just these few things and our unaided will? Or what if I had a column! I've always wanted a column. I bet if I proposed a column about desert island life someone would print it for sure. I bet it would become syndicated. And then they'd pay me, but I'd take my pay in stuff we needed and have them ship it here. Because it'd be hard not to have books, I'm thinking now. This is getting a little more complicated than I had in mind, my husband said. I was thinking that the whole point of the desert island thing was letting go of stuff. But wouldn't you like a couple of records?

I asked. Yeah, I would like a few records, he said. But then we'd have to bring something to play them on. That's true. Wouldn't it be nicer if we just sang to each other? That would be nice, I have to admit. You have a good voice, he said. And if we did that, couldn't we also tell each other stories? We could make up new ones, or try to remember the stories and books we loved. That sounds great, I said, but I still think I want to bring some sewing. How about if we bring as many things as we want, I said. I'm not sure that would really enhance the desert island feeling, he said. Well, we'd still be deserted, I said. Yes, but the point is to experience life, real life. I'm not so sure about this desert island thing, I said. Maybe the woods would be a better choice, we could have electricity and all the amenities and we wouldn't have to worry about all the shipping. I like the woods, he said. Why do people romanticize being stranded on a desert island so much, anyway, I said. Because it would be just the two of us, he said. That would be sexy. But it's just the two of us now, I said. It's sexy now. Yeah, except for the whole world thing, he said. Right, the world. That can be a pain, I said. What if, instead of being on a desert island, we just made the whole world go away? So, what, we'd be stranded in space instead? No, I mean, keep the world, make all the people go away. Yes! I said, *That* could be cool. How would we make them all go away without killing them? No, they'd just be gone. Just the same way we'd just be on the desert island. We'd just wake up and they'd be gone and we'd be like, Wow, everyone's gone. Everything is ours. We'd be the richest, most famous people in the world. We'd be the most everything in the world. The most whatever we wanted to be, he said. That seems like maybe too much responsibility, I said. People aren't so bad. I like a lot of them. We could make more, he said. I think the desert island seems kind of the more simple way to go, I said. It just depends what you want, he said. Would you rather have everything, or nothing?

PROMISE

I WILL FEED YOU SUGAR.

I will not name you anything like Kal-El or Pilot Inspektor, but I might think about it for a minute. I will name you something different, but not too different. I will not paint your room blue or pink whatever sex you are, even though I like blue and pink. Your room will not have a theme. You will not know who Barney is until there is no remote chance that you will care. I will plug up all the plugs, put away all the cords, lock up all the cabinets, pack up all the breakable thingies, keep the medicine locked up, I will direct you away from hot things, I will cover the sharp edges on the furniture. Or, we'll just move. We'll move to an apartment with no edges of any kind, with outlets up around waist high, we'll get beanbag furniture. I will still forget something, but even if I don't, you will fall down, and when you fall down, I will hate myself for a little while. When you cry, I will pick you up, but if you cry too long or too loud or in a weird way, I won't like it. I am not opposed to the use of a pacifier, but I will never call it a binky. When you make six poops a day, I will not complain about your diapers but I will probably call you stink-maker to your face. I will look at your poops closely. I will tell your father what color and size and shape they are. Every day. We are practicing for this now. After your bath I will slather you with smelly-goody things. Without a doubt I will kiss your butt. When you are bigger and tired of poop in your pants I will teach you how to use the potty. I will say, *It's easy! Sit on the seat! Poop and pee!* You will see how easy it is.

I will not talk to you in a baby voice, but I will sing to you in a silly voice. I will never, ever, ever talk down to you. I will try not to, but I am likely to swear at some point. I will feed you mashed-up peas and beets and chicken and whatever, but you will know what cake is, because cake is good and anyway no way in hell will you be one of those two-hundred-pound talk-show babies, not on my watch. When you get the cake all over your face, I will take your picture.

When you wake up crying six times during the night, I will pick you up three times and your daddy will take over when I start to cry myself. During this period when you are crying six times during the night, I will be a little edgy during the day. Try to understand that I do not know what you are crying about. That I will wonder if your pj's itch, or if you're allergic to our laundry detergent or the sound of my voice, or if you miss the mommy who carried you, and how could you not? That I will wonder if you somehow already have a sense of the world we are trying to raise you in even though your whole world is soft and colorful and warm and smells so good all the time. Yes, I know, hungry and wet are the likely culprits, but since you won't stop when I feed and change you, what the hell? When you wake up every day at five a.m. for good, I will get up, because what else would I do?

You will need to let me read a book at some point, or I will completely freak.

I will have a shelf full of books about babies and parenting, but I will not read them. I will look at them only when you are screaming at the top of your lungs, and since it's hard to read with a baby screaming at the top of his or her lungs, I will tell the book to bite me. I will teach you by example. I will teach you some things I do not mean to teach you just like my mom did. I do not know in advance what those will be. You will grow up to be awesome, but flawed. If you end up in therapy, I will try to realize that's probably better than if you didn't, but I will still blame myself for that and for other things, like the war in Iraq.

You will be so super-styley. If you are twins, you will never ever ever match. You won't even coordinate. If you are twins, you will clash. You might even clash with your own self. Even if we shop exclusively at the thrift store, I will pull T-shirts over your little head and you might fuss, but when you're dressed I'll hold you up in the mirror and you will think in your baby thoughts, *I look good.* When you give me time, I will sew you things. Give me time.

No way will I carry anything that even remotely resembles a diaper bag, not even a Kate Spade diaper bag that's supposed to look fancy but only looks like a diaper bag that cost a lot of money. I don't know what to do about the stroller situation. I will find the least strollery-looking stroller. I will wheel you around on a dolly. I will not talk about diaper genies. I will never say *diaper genie* in conversation to anyone. I will not be a cliché. I will be a cliché. I won't. Your mommy will be so punk.

When you learn to walk, I will hold your hands. When you learn to run and you run straight into the oven door, I will take you to the hospital to get stitches. At the hospital I will yell at people randomly, officially marking my complete transformation into my own mother.

I will not make you take a picture at Sears Portrait Studio, ever. But I will take your picture at home, often. I will document your every first: your first smile, your first steps, the first time you seem like you're about to hold a bottle even if what you're really trying to do is throw it to the floor for the first time. I will document your first sneeze. How I will capture your first sneeze is I will have just taken a photo of you that I thought was your first yawn of the new year, but which was actually you starting to sneeze.

When you come home, I will whisper my promise to tell you all about where you came from someday.

In the winter I will dress you up in a snowsuit and take you to the park. I will never, not for one second, take my eyes off you. When I scope out possible predators, it will be from the eyes in the back of my head. Oh, and don't think they're not there.

I will want you to have only wooden, beautiful toys, or handmade stuffed animals, or one-of-a-kind antique dolls, but that will not happen. So I will make you put your plastic toys in a wooden bucket. I will try to get you toys that you want, but I will simultaneously be trying to recreate my own childhood, or possibly the childhood I want now, so I hope, if you are a boy, that you will not be too upset about the amount of Hello Kitty things I bring home.

I will never let you get too cold or too hot or wet. I will tell you how much god loves you. I will tell you that god made you so smart and beautiful and talented and good and that you can grow up to be whatever you want, but I will not let you be on *America's Most Talented Kids*. You will not have to run away to be a circus performer because I will let you be a circus performer locally.

I will say no to you. However much I say no to you, you will think you won't like it but really you will.

In autumn, I will walk down the street with you in a Snugli, in that outfit your daddy likes (jean jacket, jeans, boots, long wooly scarf), and I will wear big sunglasses and carry takeout coffee in one hand and a bag from Barney's in the other and I will take long strides just like Meg Ryan or Angelina Jolie or Nicole Kidman, except no one will be taking our picture and what will be in the Barney's bag is a baggie full of Cheerios. Which we will share.

I will explain to you, as soon as you have a word or two, that another mommy carried you in her tummy. When you have a few more words I will explain that that mommy loved you so much she knew we had the most love to give you. Or something. I will explain to you why we look different. Even if you are the same color, or are a pale shade of freckled ivory similar to my own, I will not ever try to say I don't see color when I see people. How could I not see color in people if I see it in T-shirts and fruit? I see color fine. I will try to remind you of where you came from and where you are now just the right amount. It might be hard for me to learn Chinese or Russian at this point, but I will learn a few words and try to remember to ask you if you want some shui-goo or if you want to come to the yin-hang with me. I will make sure you know that you are in the right home. I will try to put the exact right amount of Guatemalan or Ethiopian things in your room, enough so you know where you came from but not so many that you forget where you are. I will say the exact right thing. I will try to say the exact right thing. If I say the exact wrong thing, I will have meant the exact right thing. Know that now.

When you get old enough to start spilling things, I will be so bummed at first, and I will sigh loudly and say, *It's okay, it happens*, and you will know from my tone that I don't think it's okay, especially after you spilled coffee on my favorite cardigan, but it really is okay, and after a while I will stop wearing my favorite cardigans, but I will not start wearing giant college sweatshirts and mom jeans, never. I promise always to be a hot mom. Even if I'm the oldest mom at your school, I will always be a hot mom. Unless you don't want me to be a hot mom. Then I'll try only to be a hot mom away from your school, or I'll drop you off across the street, but I will still watch you until you get inside.

Dinner will be disappointing, but we will all sit down at the table together and there will be something on it three to five times a week. You will not grow up to be a person who eats something in a restaurant and says, *This isn't how my mom used to make it*, because chances are high that Mom never made it at all. I will learn to make your grandmother's Frito casserole. That's good stuff. Two to four times a week, when there's too much mail piled up on the table, we will eat somewhere else, like our bed, and the TV might be on. Get used to it.

I will watch *Wallace & Gromit* with you 587 times. You will watch TV. If anyone tells you TV makes you stupid or ruins your life, you tell them your mommy watches TV and she wrote three books and teaches college. You tell them that people who watch TV also read books. I will read you a lot of books. I will read you books before you are even born, I will read you books when you are so young all you probably hear is, *Eerh lala hrrm mmm hm ha ha*, I will read you enough books so that you will know how to read when you are one, probably, and then I will read you more books. And even if you can read when you are one and you are the most genius kid ever, you will not be one of those six-year-olds who goes to college, because that's just not right.

If some kid tries to bully you in school, I will tell you to invite her over and I will bring you Slice and bake cookies and I won't say anything but I will look her in the eye and scare the shit out of her while I'm handing her a glass of milk and smiling in her face and trust me she will never bully you again. If you show any signs of being a bully to anyone, let me just tell you right now we're not having any of that. You will say please and thank you. You will send thank-you notes as soon as you can write. People like thank-you notes.

I will know the names of your teachers and whether you like them or not. I will care about your grades, but I will not make you feel bad about a C or a B-plus or an A-minus. No one should ever feel bad about an A-minus. If you get a C-minus or a D, I will spend more time helping you with your homework. When you are in eighth grade, I will no longer be able to help you with your math homework, so if your dad can't help you with it, I will get you a tutor. When you are in tenth grade, I will no longer be able to help you with your science homework. When you are in AP History, I will be really, really impressed and tell you so. If you decide you might be a writer, I will be very helpful.

We will play a variety of rock and roll music, classical music, and kids music—if there's any such thing that's not super corny—around the house from the time you come into it. If you start listening to some loud music that I find excruciating when you're twelve or thirteen—I don't know what, country or boy bands—I will make you close the door. Whatever it is, I will be like every other parent in history and think that the music from our day was better.

If you want to wear a trench coat every day, that's cool, but if you hoard ammo in the garage, I will not pretend that's not fucked up. If you start smoking cigarettes, ever, I will try to have a rational conversation about it, but if you keep it up, you will not win the fight.

If you ever say, *You're not my real mom*, I will try not to flinch, I will tell myself things about *just words, just words*, but this will crush me. If you ever, ever, ever tell me you hate me or your daddy for any reason, that is just not gonna fly. I will tell you to tell me to go fuck myself before you use the word *hate*, ever, to us or to anyone, and if you say, *Fine, go fuck yourself,* do not plan events outside of your room for an undetermined length of time.

If you are a girl and you kiss a boy in first grade, I will refer you to your father. If you kiss a boy your senior year of high school and it sucks, I will tell you it gets better later. If you are a boy and you kiss a girl ever, I will first tell you how not to become a jerk down the line and it might be obvious that I've had some issues and then I will refer you to your father. If you are a boy and you want to kiss boys or if you are a girl and you kiss a girl in tenth grade and it rocks your world, I will say, *Right on*, even though you will tell me that people have stopped using that phrase. I will tell you about the birds and the bees with plenty of advance notice, but I will not involve any birds and bees in this story.

Once in a while, I will leave something out that you shouldn't see.

Occasionally, I will embarrass you.

I will, inevitably and without meaning to, send you a mixed message. I will not pick up after you when you are old enough to pick up after yourself, but if you see me picking up after Daddy, I might not have a good explanation. If you see me eating cookies before dinner, I will try very very hard not to explain it by saying anything that remotely translates to, *Because I'm the mommy, that's why*. I will say that I am eighty percent consistent and you will not think I'm as funny as I do.

When you experiment with drugs, I will have thought about what to do for the previous fourteen years, and I will still not know what to say when you remind me that I experimented with drugs too. I will want to say, *And that is how I know you should not experiment with drugs,* but I will know that this will not help my case. I will want to find the way to be most cool about it, but I will not realize that this is really not possible.

I will try to stay out of your love life, but I will urge you to practice the safe sex I do not want to hear details about, ever. And if your girlfriend calls you names or your boyfriend hits you, I will kick their fucking asses down the stairs and out the door.

Aw, hell yeah! I will monitor your Internet use or whatever the kids are using when you're that age. I will monitor the chip in your head. Brain-chip predators coming around my kid will regret it.

When you go away to college, I will know that you are doing things I wish you weren't doing, but I will try to muster some denial about it.

If you go through a period in your twenties of making one terrible choice after another, I will try not to tell you it'll get better in about ten years. Even though it's true. I will try to let you make your own mistakes, I will try not to get into a shouting match with you if I find out you don't have health insurance, or if you date a series of emotionally unavailable actor/poets, or if you move across country and back in a single week, or if you do anything else I've done myself and therefore know is a terrible, terrible mistake. If you remain single until you're forty-one, or forever, I will not think something is wrong with you. I will never think anything is wrong with you.

When you become the last thing in the world I thought you'd become—an accountant, or a school bus driver, or a marine biologist—and it makes you really, really happy, I will be really, really happy. When you get a plaque that says *Accountant* or *School Bus Driver* or *Marine Biologist of the Year*, I will write about it in the holiday letter. When you get pregnant but you don't want to get married because marriage is a meaningless construct of society, I will write about it in the holiday letter. When I become a grandma, I will meddle, I will spoil your children and let you suffer the consequences, I will write about my grandkids' speed-walking races or sixth-place 4-H ribbons in the holiday letter.

Someday, you might have to change my diapers, or maybe your dad's. Just remember: we did it for you.

I will do all of this. I will do none of this. I will love you so hard.

If I think I won't see you again, I will kiss your face and say, *It was really nice knowing you.*

ELIZABETH CRANE is the author of two previous collections of short stories from Little, Brown: *When the Messenger Is Hot* and *All This Heavenly Glory*. Her work has been featured in *Other Voices*, *Mississippi Review*, *Bridge*, the *Chicago Reader*, the *Believer*, and several anthologies including *McSweeney's Future Dictionary of America*, *The Best Underground Fiction*, *Loser*, *Altared*, and *The Show I'll Never Forget*. She is also a regular contributor to *Writer's Block Party* on WBEZ Chicago. In 2003 she received the Chicago Public Library 21st Century Award. She currently teaches creative writing and lives in Chicago with her husband Ben and their dog Percival Fontaine Barksdale Brandt.